Books by Bill Thesken

Blocking Paris
The Lords of Xibalba
Window

The
Oil Eater

Bill Thesken

Copyright © 2013 Bill Thesken

First Edition Published 2013

Koloa Publishing, LLC

P.O. Box 1609

Koloa, HI 96756

ISBN 978-0-615-90718-5

ISBN 0615907180

bi·o·re·me·di·a·tion–
n.

The use of living organisms, such as plants or bacteria, to neutralize or eliminate contaminants in polluted soil or water.

2013 Global proved oil reserves: 350 billion barrels@42 Gallons per Barrel = Fourteen trillion seven hundred billion gallons of oil.

One gallon of oil can contaminate one million gallons of water.

1.

Abigail Campbell was claustrophobic.

One day when she was five years old and in kindergarten the meanest kid in school locked her in a coat closet right before the class went to recess, just shoved her right in there and locked the door, and with all the commotion of thirty little kids running out to the playground, no one heard her yelling for help, and no one knew she was missing for close to half an hour. When the teacher finally found her she was just a little ball of sobbing tears on the bottom of the closet.

That was twenty two years ago, and while most of that frightful experience like most of her childhood itself had rubbed off on the millstone of her life, some inklings of that fear never really went away, they just got swept under the carpet of her existence.

Riding in elevators scared the hell out of her. She couldn't sit in a car with the windows up. A walk-in closet was out of the question.

And here she was in a damn submarine, a small one at that, and even though the entire sub was the size of a small bus, the cabin was just about as big as the inside of a Volkswagen Beetle, with the windows up. She tried to breathe normal but her lungs were tight and her heart was fluttering and felt like it was about to burst out of her chest. She closed her eyes for a moment and settled herself, imagining that she was in a giant forest with towering green trees, blue sky with fluffy white clouds, a cool stream was nearby, and the world around her was huge.

When she opened her eyes again she was still in the capsule that seemed no bigger than that coat closet from long ago.

They were headed for the bottom.

Three thousand feet below the surface and descending, the little submarine began to creak as the metal frame adjusted to the crushing weight of the half mile column of water above it. Flood lamps on the hull cast eerie beams of lights through the dark water illuminating the bits of plankton like snowflakes on a winter's night floating in the black depths of the ocean.

She never told anyone she was afraid of tight spaces, if she had she never would have gotten anywhere near this expedition, and her whole career to this point in time hinged on it.

Drops of sweat formed on her forehead as she peered out the window and she used the back of her hand to wipe away the moisture, and whispered softly to herself. "Why did I sign up for this trip?"

The skipper of the two man submersible looked over at her with concern, then smiled. "For the science Abby, or at least that's what you told me this morning when we went over the final briefing. I ask everyone the same question before we squeeze into this little ship, why do you want to go under water, and why do you want to go so very far under water. Everyone who gets the nod to go on this vessel gets a thorough check up, mental, physical, it's almost like going on a mission to outer space with NASA, testing and testing and testing, but I always like to get in the last needle so to speak, so if anyone has a touch of the wiggies, I'll see it and scrub the mission on the spot. You came through with flying colors and that's why you're here and not Dr. Nelson. Now about this particular hot smoker vent that we're heading down to see, I understand from the unmanned submersible data and the sonar we've collected that these things have been here for hundreds, perhaps thousands of years. There's a little hole in the earth's crust and these things are like little volcanoes, and the crust is just rolling right over it."

He was talking in long slow sentences as he did to all his passengers when he sensed a little panic in their tone of voice, telling them the worst of it all, and then soothing them. Of course it was terrifying going this deep under water. They could be crushed at any moment.

"Salt water has forty four hundredths pounds per square inch per foot of depth," she said. "At three thousand feet the pressure on the hull is currently one thousand three hundred twenty pounds per square inch."

The skipper shook his head. "You forgot the atmosphere above the ocean."

She laughed nervously. "Oh right; plus an extra fourteen point seven pounds of pressure for the atmosphere, so it's one thousand three hundred thirty four point seven pounds per square inch. By the time we get to our destination of four thousand five hundred feet, the pressure on the hull will be..ah…one thousand nine hundred and seven pounds per square inch. That's like a small truck parked on every square inch of this hull."

The Captain smiled. "So it's true what they say, you really are a walking calculator. But you think too much Abby. Relax, and enjoy the ride. This hull…" he tapped on the window, "can withstand ten times that pressure."

She wiped another drop of sweat off her forehead and winced. The walking calculator. She got that nickname in her first year of pre med and somehow it stuck no matter how hard she tried to squash it. And now it had followed her to the depths of the ocean in a creaky little can with a grey haired retired US Navy sub captain.

"So what about you", she asked, trying to shake her nerves. "What's your nickname? Surely you must have one, being in the Navy all those years, don't all you guys have nicknames?"

"Thirty years in the force, promoted to Captain when I was forty years old. I commanded two nuclear subs, and one battleship in seven years worth of tours around the globe, kept the crews and boats safe, and never a mishap. You always have to stay ahead of the curve when you

4

have a billion dollar piece of equipment in your care. Surround yourself with good people, keep morale high, feed 'em well, and it works like a fine tuned clock. Then I had shore duty for a few tours, passed over for Admiral three years in a row, and so I got out. I retired at fifty five years of age."

"You didn't answer my question."

"Sure, I had plenty of nicknames over the years in the Navy. From Swabbie in the beginning to Old Iron lips at the end, and a bunch of unmentionable ones in the middle I'm sure."

She laughed. "Old Iron lips? Isn't it normally Old Iron sides?"

"You have to understand, getting promoted to Admiral is very, let's say, political. In other words you have to kiss a lot of rear ends," he turned to her and winked, "pardon me Abby. You see there's a lot of waste in the bureaucracy of the United States armed forces. A lot of wasted money going places it has no right to go. I saw it firsthand. I called them on it, and made a lot of enemies. I wouldn't so to speak 'pucker up' to keep the status quo, and so my buddies named me Old Iron lips."

"Guys are funny."

"Yeah, but it all worked out great. I was hired by this research company to drive their twenty million dollar sub, I have a full pension plus this pay, and my wife is happy since I'm not milling around the house and getting in her way every day."

A long, slow groaning noise filled the cabin and echoed throughout the hull. Abby's eyes widened and she gently touched the round glass bubble that stretched over the whole cabin and gave them a one hundred eighty degree view of pitch black terror.

"It's just the metal in the bottom part of the hull," the skipper said, "adjusting to the pressure. The glass bubble is solid as a rock."

He winked at her. "Borosilicate glass, the same kind of glass you use for those beakers in your laboratories." He tapped on the bubble. "Two layers, each one four and half inches thick. It actually gets stronger the more pressure that's exerted on it. There is something about the round shape and compression. It's been tested to forty five thousand feet worth of pressure, and that is way down there my friend. We're only going about five thousand feet today."

"How do you test it to forty five thousand feet, when the deepest point of the ocean is thirty six thousand feet?"

"Pressure chamber built specifically to test this sub. The pressure chamber alone cost two million to build, but think about it, if you're going to put twenty million bucks into a submarine, you may as well test it before you put someone in it, right?"

"Amen to that," she agreed.

The submarine measured twenty five feet in length, ten feet wide, and ten feet high, with a pontoon ballast on each side. The glass dome over their heads measured eight feet wide and four feet high, like a big clear ball cut in half and attached to the top of the sub. The owners of the sub were a lively bunch, and had the name 'Minnow' painted on the side.

The skipper was comfortable being in command. His eyes scanned the gauges arrayed on the dash board in front of him and he maneuvered the craft with the joystick and foot pedals as in a helicopter, keeping the sub level as they sank through the water. He clicked a red button on the stick and spoke into the headset.

"Minnow to Base, over." There was a silent pause, and then the radio crackled on the speakers inside the cabin.

"Base to Minnow go ahead, over."

"All is well. We're descending at a rate of one hundred feet per minute. Current depth is three four three five and counting. We should reach the target in fifteen minutes."

They were in the Bathypelagic zone, otherwise known as the midnight zone, a depth of the ocean that extended from three thousand feet to thirteen thousand feet below the surface. No light penetrated to these depths. The next stop was the Abyssopelagic zone, simply known as the Abyss, but they weren't heading that far today.

The skipper tapped on a gauge on the console. "Water temperature forty one degrees." He turned to Abby. "We have a ways to go before it freezes."

"Sea water freezes at twenty eight point four

degrees Fahrenheit", she mumbled. "And as it gets closer to the freezing point it gets denser."

Great, she thought, just what they needed, denser water.

Five miles off the Galapagos island of San Cristobal, they were heading to the bottom of the ocean, into an area known to have black sea smokers, hydrothermal vents in the earth's crust that expelled mineral rich magma heated water at temperatures of up to eight hundred sixty seventy degrees Fahrenheit. Where this super heated water mixed with the cold water at crushing depths, there existed a strange temperate zone that was sometimes full of life.

Chemoautotrophic bacteria thrived in this hostile neighborhood, feeding off of the sulfur compounds and hydrogen sulfide to produce a type of organic material through chemosynthesis. The bacteria form a thick mat on the surface near the vents. Amphipods and copepods, like little underwater fleas, feed on the bacterial mat, and then shrimp, fish, crabs and octopi feed on the fleas. Giant six foot high tube worms absorb the nutrients from the bacteria in their tissue. The bacterium was the organic key to an entire ecosystem, a keystone species.

"I can't believe I'm almost there," she whispered as she looked beneath the ship, the thrill of it erasing her claustrophobia. "Two years of waiting, plotting, coercing, pleading, I did everything except rob a bank to get here."

He looked at her with renewed respect. "I

didn't know scientists were so conniving."

"Oh, you have no idea the battles it took to get the funding for this expedition. Our little dive is costing the university a cool quarter million dollars. For thirty minutes on the bottom, that's like eight thousand three hundred thirty three dollars per minute."

"Plus tip," he added.

She laughed, and then got serious. "I just have to get a clean pressurized sample of that bacteria mat."

He shook his head. "I just can't get over how a girl that looks like you could get so wrapped up in the exciting world of microbiology. You look like you could be a model Abby, or be in the movies."

"If I had a dime for every time I heard that skipper, I could buy a sub like this instead of renting it."

"Sorry."

"It's just fascinating," she said. "The smallest of living creatures is the keystone for life on our entire planet. The bacteria that I'm going after could give us a look at what life is like on other planets, or cure the common cold, I don't know. Crushing pressure, no light, toxic minerals, searing heat, and yet life. It goes against all common knowledge. What I'm after is the most extreme life on the planet, and I have to find out what makes it tick."

"So what are you going to do with these bacteria, if, and when you find them?"

She smiled, happy to talk about it. "Once I have it back at the lab, I'm going to separate, and isolate the DNA, and compare it with other types of bacteria. I'll experiment on it, put it through some tests, and subject it to some extreme conditions. I have a theory that this particular type of bacteria is descended from the first life on our planet, and that someday we're going to find strains of it on other planets."

He narrowed his skeptical brow, and looked at her as though she had just escaped from the funny farm.

She frowned as she saw the look on his face and continued. "I know it may sound crazy, but I'm going to subject the bacteria to conditions found on Venus, Triton, Mars, and Jupiter. I'll duplicate the chemical makeup and pressure of the atmospheres on those planets. We'll tinker with the DNA, grow it, and mold it."

"Well you better get ready Abby, because we're almost there."

She caught her breath and looked out the bubble. The lights from the hull were shining down on a surreal scene. They were approaching a rubble strewn surface scattered with twisted chimneys spouting black smoky water. Their descent slowed to a crawl and they hovered fifty feet above the bottom.

The captain clicked the mic. "Minnow to base, we've reached the bottom. We'll visually scan the area and begin sample collection."

The radio crackled back. "Roger Minnow."

They came to a stop, suspended twenty feet above a line of smokers that spread off into the darkness. The skipper maneuvered the craft with the joystick and brought the craft up stream of the black smoke. He kept one eye on the dials, and one eye on the bottom.

"The current's running about two knots, not bad. We should be able to get pretty close once you decide which one you want to try for."

Abby was like a kid in a candy store, all fear had washed away. Spread out below them was a vast array of life stretching into the distance.

The chimneys were steadily churning out black clouds of smoke, and growing everywhere alongside of them were colorful tube worms, six feet in height with their red feathered tongues extended to catch plankton and whatever else they could get a hold of. Spider like crabs scampered about, shrimp and strange shaped fish darted around the black plumes of super heated water staying just out of its reach.

"Okay," the skipper said, "Go ahead Abby and get the robotic arms ready"

She had been practicing with a simulator for the past couple of weeks, but that was at the surface, in an air conditioned lab. Now she had a mile's worth of water on her head. She powered up the robot arms with a flick of a switch, and extended them slowly straight out from the hull using the toggle controls that looked a typical computer gaming device.

She chuckled. "And Daddy used to say

playing computer games was a waste of time."

The arm on the right was the scooper grabber tool, about the size of a hand, and built like a shovel, with fingers that clamped over with hinges. She swiveled it and rotated the hand, clamping the fingers twice. The arm on the left held the pressure capsule, a gallon sized titanium jar with a hinged lid that locked with a twist. There were seven additional jars attached to the hull and the plan was to fill each one with a sample.

She scanned the scene below and then pointed to the right. "Over there, the big smoker with the two smaller ones on the sides, like a trident spear."

The skipper looked down and around, checked the surrounding area and nodded while keeping the sub motionless.

"Just to review," he reminded her. "You'll have the robot arms pulled back to the hull, and I'll approach the target. The arms are ten feet long. I'll get us within seven feet of the target, and then you'll extend the arms for the collection, got it?"

"Got it", she nodded eagerly, and pulled the arms back to the sub.

"Okay, we're heading in."

He slowly maneuvered the sub down and towards the trident chimney. The main chimney structure rose fifteen feet from the bottom and was a jumbled mass of solidified sulfide minerals. The sub stopped and hovered, and Abby extended the robot arms. The skipper toggled a switch and rotated a beam of light directly at her target; a mass of bacteria that looked like thick white slime was located directly below the bellowing vent. Using the robot scooper like a hand she gently scraped it along the chimney gathering bacterial mat and rock and shoveled it into the metal jar.

Two more scoops and it was full, and she twisted the jar closed and brought it back to the sub and attached it to the side with a snap lever.

For the next twenty minutes they floated alongside the smoker methodically gathering tubeworms and bacteria. Seven jars were filled and they were working on the eighth and final sample.

Abby extended the robot arm towards one of the smaller chimneys on the side of the large one, and began scooping material and creatures.

The sub, motionless for the most part suddenly lurched a few inches forward with the current and the robot hand broke through the chimney.

"Damn," the skipper muttered.

The robot hand was embedded in the chimney. Small puffs of black smoke crept out from around the scooper.

Abby gently toggled the controller to pull back the arm, but it was no use. She tried to swivel the hand but it did not move. It was stuck in the hole it had made.

"Now what?" she asked.

"Let me think," the skipper whispered. "We

don't want to force it and lose the arm, that's a fifty thousand dollar piece of equipment. On the other hand, we don't want to be stuck here forever."

He hissed through his teeth and bit his lower lip as he studied the situation.

"Alright, now try rocking the arm up and down as you pivot the hand. Little movements now and try to widen that hole a bit."

She began rocking the arm, and then pivoting the hand.

"Easy now," he pleaded. "Now slowly pull back on the arm…"

The sub was being pulled towards the chimney as she pulled the arm back and he toggled the thrusters on the hull to keep the sub from smashing into the rock.

The chimney suddenly broke apart and as the hand came free black smoke and super heated water jetted towards them from the gaping hole enveloping the sub as it retreated.

There was a snapping sound like a tray of breaking ice from the freezer, and the hair stood up on the back of Abby's neck. A four foot long crack was suddenly in the glass shell in front of her terrified eyes.

The skipper barked into the head set. "Code red, heading for the surface." He flicked a switch that jettisoned the iron weights on the bottom of the hull and the sub began a fast ascent, the smokers quickly fading from view.

Abby couldn't breathe and her heart seemed

to stop beating. A voice inside her brain was yelling, "Get me out of here, get me out of here!"

"It's the outer shell," the skipper said in a calm and soothing voice. "We'll be okay."

"What happened?" Abby was breathing again and trying not to hyperventilate.

"The shell is made from borosilicate glass which is super strong. However it does not like abrupt changes in temperature, it will crack but it won't shatter. The water temperature was a steady thirty eight degrees, and that jet of molten water was somewhere around…"

"Five hundred degrees," she finished for him.

"Yeah, that's a big change."

The sub shook as it climbed through the thick black water. Abby gripped the arms of the chair, voiceless.

The skipper toggled the mike and spoke into it. "Base over."

The speaker crackled. "Base to Minnow, what's the situation?'

"Base we have a cracked outer windshield, no seepage. This is an emergency ascent, please clear the area and confirm."

"Roger Minnow we're tracking you on sonar a thousand yards directly off our bow. We'll launch the rescue craft."

He turned to Abby. "Three hundred feet per minute, it's about as fast as we can go. We'll be at the surface pretty quick."

The black water slowly began to lighten as they rose. Deep swimming schools of fish, and a manta ray flashed by in the distance, clouds of jellyfish swirled by the window.

The ascent began to slow as they got closer to the surface and the pressure in the cabin began to match the pressure in the water, and then they could see the shimmering surface of the water appear in the distance above them.

Two hundred feet, then one hundred feet, and then the sub burst out of the sea into the air like a cork and settled back on the surface.

Abby looked out at the blue sky, the water shedding off the cracked borosilicate bubble, like the tears from her eyes, and the rescue craft racing towards them, and she finally let out a sigh of relief.

2.

Jonah MacLean stood tall and breathed in a long and deep breath, relishing the pine scented northern air and surveyed his surroundings. His thick beard shrouded the smile on his face, and his piercing blue eyes twinkled with mirth. No matter what the circumstances, or what was about to happen he was thinking, it was great to be alive. As long as you're still breathing, you've got a chance.

It was early in the summer on the shores of Rock Island in the Gulf of Alaska. The air was crisp and clear and had a crackle in it, with the pine trees shining in the sun, a bald eagle floated lazily up high in the blue sky searching the water below for prey.

He was standing on the shore of a small uninhabited island in the fjords of Alaska. It was a rugged area of mountains, rocks, forest, and glaciers. Rising from the water nearby were other small islands, and the mainland notched with crags and bays indiscriminate from the islands meandered in the distance creating the illusion that he was on a great northern lake surrounded by forest. In fact he was in a bay near the entrance to Prince William Sound on the southern coast of Alaska, and it was the briny waters from the great North Pacific Ocean that lapped gently against the shore.

He walked across the rounded cobblestones into the cold water till the ocean was near the tops of his waders. As he took another deep breath his shrouded smile faded and the twinkle in his eyes was replaced with a flash of anger, for mingled now with the scent of fresh pine and salt was the faint acrid aroma of crude oil.

Early this morning an oil tanker cruising at full speed hit a submerged shipping container in the Sound and twenty thousand gallons of Prudhoe Bay crude leaked out of the hull. A slick the size of Manhattan was spreading towards this little island like an advancing army, the waves of oil tar bobbing in the swell just over the horizon. The once pristine blue water would soon be streaked inky white as the oil and water that were never intended to meet, mixed into a toxic brew. Thousands of dead fish would float on the water, and oil covered birds would struggle to the shore or worse, their feathers covered with black slime and weighing them down to their death.

It was an all too familiar sight and it always put a knot in the pit of his stomach. When he was twelve years old the Exxon Valdez oil tanker went aground on Bligh Reef in the Sound. Twenty five million gallons of crude oil were spilled into the ocean and covered thirteen hundred miles of coastline. Thousands of Alaskan residents as well as many from nearby Canada and other states volunteered to help with the cleanup, and so his

Dad signed them up and they spent the summer scrubbing beaches and birds. When he first heard that he was going to Alaska to help with the cleanup, his pre-teen mentality thought of high adventure in the wilderness. It turned out to be the most excruciating and horrible thing he had ever seen. Thousands of birds, otters, and seals and fish and crabs were dying from being covered in the oil, rotting on the beaches or struggling to stay alive. The stench was overwhelming, and they did the best they could with what they had.

When they got home from Alaska, Jonah dove straight into books and school and never looked back. He was determined to be the best chemist on the planet and figure out a better way to clean up these types of disasters. Twenty five years later, and now thirty seven years old, he was still trying to find a solution.

The company he worked for specialized in oil spills and he had seen his fair share. As the senior scientist at O'Malley Bioremedial his job was to oversee the production and implementation of products to clean up the grimy mess. They were a new company, and they were on their way up. They were the first ones on the scene, and the last to leave. In some cases they would never leave, and just monitor the situation for years.

When an oil spill occurred on water the first method of containment was floating booms, like those little floaties that kids took to the beach, thousands of them all strung together to rope and corral the oil in one area. If the concentration was high enough they could burn the surface oil which in itself was a nasty business. Or they could suck up the surface oil with giant vacuums and separate the oil from the water with filters.

Another method was chemical dispersants which separated the oil particles to make them easier to assimilate with the volume of water and made it easier for the natural bacteria to attach itself and eat it. That however was the worst alternative since the disbursement agents were sometimes more toxic that the oil itself.

The last and best alternative was employing billions of tiny microbes to gobble up the oil. And that's where he came in. Crude oil is a naturally occurring substance, and as such there are many areas in the world where it just seeps right out of the earth through cracks in the surface. Nature being what it is, adapting life to an environment; strains of bacteria evolved over time to take advantage of the carbon energy in the crude oil. He would search out and find these pockets of naturally occurring seepages and collect the bacteria on the fringes. Back at the lab they would cultivate and grow the bacteria until they had vast quantities, thousands of gallons of the little critters, and different types for different situations. There were those suited for salt water, fresh water, brackish water, sandy soils, and marshes.

As fate would have it, he was on a fishing vacation on a nearby lake when the tanker hit the container. He was burned out from research and needed a break, so he loaded up his little seaplane and flew up from Seattle, winding along the coast of British Columbia, stopping at Ketchikan, and then Valdez to refuel, and then landing at the secluded inland lake after a full day in the air. He loved to fly, it was freedom and cruising over empty wooded terrain was a relief. One hundred miles north of Valdez there were thousands of small lakes and he would just fly and fly until he found one that looked good and landed, swooping from the sky and skimming to a stop on the surface. And then he would just drift and fish from the seaplanes pontoons. The quiet ripples lapping on the hulls, broken only by the distant wail of a moose, or the screech of an eagle in flight. The trout and pike were aggressive and attacked the lures with ferocity, the tip of the hooks barely touching the water from his cast when a geyser of water would explode, his pole bent in half, line screaming from the reel.

It was on one such strike when his cell phone rang. He was fighting a big one, coaxing it to the plane, the line would scream out, and then he'd wind it back in, over and over, and as the fish got closer it spotted him on the pontoon and got spooked and ran deep, he looked over towards the ringing phone in the cockpit and the line broke.

"That was a good battle" he sighed, and reached in to take the call.

Thirty minutes later he was flying over the tanker. Rescue boats from nearby Valdez were on the scene. A ring of containment floats circled the break in the hull, but a two mile wide slick had gotten away. It was spreading south with the current and the wind, and from the air he could trace the forward trajectory which ended at the northern end of the big rock island.

His plane was now anchored next to the shore of that island and he reached down into the water and pried out a scallop that was attached to a rock. It was bigger than his hand.

Throughout the water he saw a wide variety of shellfish, scallops, crabs, shrimp and fish. He shook his head in disgust at the approaching oil.

So this is where they would make their stand. He took a close look at the pristine coastline that would soon be covered in grime. There was no time to waste. He pulled out his cell phone dialed up the office.

"O'Malley Bioremedial, can I help you?" Penny Smith was more than a pretty blonde; she was the glue that held the company together. Answering phones, packing supplies, you name it, she made it happen.

"Penny, its Jonah."

She sat up straight. "Hey boss. Where are you?"

"I'm on the ground. Knee deep in water to be more precise."

"What's the situation?"

"Not good. I flew over the spill. It's big, and headed for a nice little island that's covered with your favorite shellfish."

"Scallops." She bit her lower lip.

"I'll save some for you," he said. "Is the contract ready?"

"I'm just finishing it up. I'll have it ready in five minutes."

The insurance company for the shipping company would lose millions in environmental suits, and they were signing up cleanup crews as fast as they could to minimize their exposure.

Jonah's company was first in line for the job, and being on site as the event was unfolding was a stroke of luck, although it sickened him to see it happening.

"Okay, once it's a done deal get on the horn to Valdez, and sign up two helicopters and a transport boat. Get the crew ready, and have them load up two thousand gallons of our experimental strain."

"You sure it's ready Jonah?"

"As sure as I'll ever be."

His experimental strain was the reason he needed a break. He'd been working on it non-stop for half a year. He mixed a cold temperature bacteria they'd found on the upper steppes in Russia with one they'd found in the Dead Sea, and another from this very spot on the Sound. It took months of isolating and wrapping the DNA from the separate bacteria strains into a single super bug. The resulting engineered strain should be able to withstand lower temperatures, and salt brine conditions, and for some reason it grew and multiplied extremely fast which is what was needed when time was of the essence.

Currents and tides and wind and waves could spread an oil slick to unmanageable sizes and having a microbe that could catch it before it got out of hand was of extreme importance.

They'd know soon enough. He had done extensive testing in the lab, and secured EPA approval, but the only sure way to test these things was in the wild, in real life conditions, with tides and currents on a big spill. It was a gamble, but it was one they needed to take. His team would arrive in Valdez within eight hours, so he had some time. He went back to the plane and got a large backpack and a butter knife and got to work. Within the hour he filled up the backpack with fifty pounds of fresh pure scallops, and loaded them into the cooler with the lake trout.

There was just one more thing he needed to check on and he grabbed a long handled shovel and a test kit from the back of the plane, and waded back onto the shoreline where there was a sandy area and scooped a little soil from the top, then got out the test kit and put ten grams of soil into the beaker and added a teaspoonful of calcium oxide to dry the soil and bind any non-fuel material so it wouldn't interfere with the results, then he added a tablespoon of isopropyl alcohol and used a pump extractor to retrieve the alcohol and filtered it into the photometer. The ultra violet light of the meter shone through the filter and measured the liquid for the presence of heavy fuel oils or crude.

The meter showed no contamination, and he

grabbed the shovel and dug down two feet and repeated the test. There was a slight aberration, four parts per million. He kept digging, and the soil started turning a blackish color. When he was five feet down he repeated the test. A hundred thousand parts per million. Ten percent of the subsurface was oil. Twenty five years later, and the oil from the Exxon Valdez was still there, and everywhere else it had touched the soil, it had gone underground.

He went back to where he had gathered the scallops and scraped some of the rocks and put it through the test. Negative. It was like that all throughout the Gulf of Alaska, it was finally clean on the surface, but dig down a few feet and it was still contaminated. He loaded the cooler and gear into the plane and pushed off from the island, and was soon airborne and headed to Valdez.

Twenty miles out from the island he flew low and slow over the oil spill and then climbed. When he was at a thousand feet and on a steady course he put the plane on auto pilot and called Ross O'Malley, the owner of the company on his cell phone.

"Ross, its Jonah."

"Jonah my boy, I just got the word from Penny a while ago, I was on an international flight, and we just landed at Newark."

Jonah got right to the point. "We're going with the experimental strain."

"It's up to you Jonah, you're in charge."

"I just wanted to let you know, since it is your

company Ross, and well, there's a lot on the line, you know that. It's a high profile spill Ross, just a few miles from the Exxon Valdez site. Every newspaper in the world will be following it. It's a little dangerous, and I'm the one making the call, so it's my reputation on the chopping block so to speak, but it's your company that will ultimately have the bear the responsibility, if I'm wrong."

"I trust you Jonah. Knowing you the way I do, I don't think it's as much as a gamble as you say it might be. I know how you feel about oil spills; they hit you straight in the gut, like a punch in a fight. There's no way you're going to aim and miss something this big. If you think its ready then fire away. I'm backing you a hundred percent, and by the way it's a bit of the luck of the Irish that you just happened to be there when it happened, wouldn't you say?"

"MacLean is Scottish."

Jonah could almost see the smile on the old man's face across the phone line.

"Yes, but O'Malley is most definitely Irish."

3.

The airport at Valdez in southern Alaska is nestled between the ocean and a towering snow covered mountain range. Just a mile to the east a large glacier slowly and methodically bulldozes a winding valley through the mountains, and the rocky rubble mixed with ice feed a stream that empties into the port.

Prince William Sound has three thousand miles of coastline and one hundred fifty glaciers.

Though steadily on the march these slow moving monsters seem frozen in time, but if you look really close you can almost see them moving steadily towards the ocean. This was a favored destination for cruise liners in the summer time. The larger ships laden with tourists travelled throughout the Sound bringing their passengers in luxury to an environment where most of them wouldn't last a day on their own.

Jonah waited on the tarmac for the plane to taxi to a halt. The company leased a turbo propped cargo plane in Seattle and filled it to the brim with the tools of their trade. Two moving vans were parked next to the three helicopters he'd ordered.

As soon as the plane came to a stop, he jogged quickly over to it as a moving stairway was positioned at the doorway, and the passengers began disembarking.

Evan Murphy and his team were first off the plane. Evan was like a grip on a movie set, a jack of all trades who carried around tape and wrenches, hammers and wire, fixing and rigging equipment on the fly. If your boat broke down at sea, he could wire it back together with whatever was on deck and get you back to shore. His team of four looked like weightlifters, strong guys that could move equipment.

They all shook hands with Jonah and headed to the cargo hold on the side of the plane.

"Got everything?" Jonah asked, even though he knew that was a stupid question.

Evan smiled wryly. "Everything but the kitchen sink boss. And that's on the next plane."

Evan climbed on the forklift tongue as he rode into the air and maneuvered to the opening. They began carefully unloading the pallets onto the tarmac. Fifty gallon barrels, four to a pallet came off first, and then pallets with steel cables, tool bins, water cannons and mounts, and two strange round metal canisters half the size of a small car.

Evan ordered the pallets arranged on the asphalt, and got to work. The crew unloaded the tool bins and began attaching nozzles on the sides of the round canisters, screwing them into the threaded holes and wrenching them tight.

Next came the steel cables and they attached them to rings on the top of the canisters and unrolled the forty foot coils till they were straight. The canisters would hang down from the helicopters and spray the bacteria onto the oil slick from a height of ten feet from the surface of the water. The trigger was radio remote activated, and Evan attached the wireless device at the tops of the canisters, and threaded an electronic cable to each nozzle.

A tow vehicle attached itself to the front of the plane and it was pulled away from the staging area.

"Okay, everyone out of the area," ordered Jonah, and they all cleared out, everyone but himself and Evan remained near the canisters.

They opened a bin and took out white hazmat suits and helmets and gloves, and put them on. Evan pulled a large hose and motor over to a pallet of fifty gallon drums. Carefully opening the tuna can sized access hole on the top with a ratchet and inserting a tube that extended to the bottom of the drum and then sealed it with a lock nut to prevent any liquid from splashing out. The other end of the tube was the same design with a lock nut went into a hole in the canister with nozzles. Jonah stood next to the canister.

"Ready?" asked Evan.

Jonah nodded. "Fire it up"

Evan flicked the switch and the little motor began whirring, transferring the microbes to the first giant sprayer. Within an hour they had the sprayers loaded with the oil eaters, two hundred and fifty gallons per sprayer.

"Alright," said Jonah as he pulled off his mask. "Let's go."

The two helicopters with the sprayers dangling underneath them headed through the sky towards the spill. The plan was simple, each copter would work half the spill, spray the perimeter and zigzag into the center, then head back to the airport to refill the containers and repeat three times.

The slick was now ten miles from the stricken tanker and a Coast Guard ship had the area cleared for them and was stationed up wind from the target.

The helicopters hovered low over the oil covered surface and a fine mist sprayed from the canisters.

"C'mon guys," urged Jonah, "it's game time, make me proud."

The pilot kept the copter level watching out the window to keep the bucket just off the surface. "You talk like you've been training a team."

"In a way I have, billions and billions of little players."

The mist of bacteria laden gel settled on top of the oil sheen and the microbes went to work attaching to the globs of oil then devouring and multiplying over and over again.

Five hours later the spraying was complete and the waiting began.

Summertime in Alaska meant twenty two hours of sunlight, and when nightfall did arrive it was only dusk until the sun rose over the horizon again. It was just about impossible to sleep in these conditions, and strange to wake up a little after midnight to a sunny day. The conditions were perfect for the oil eating bacteria however, since they thrived when mixed with oxygen and sunlight.

A low pressure cell formed over South Alaska, and the winds turned dead calm. The sea became a reflecting pond, and the air hung over it like a warm blanket.

The yellow half moon rode low in the sky and the currents slowed to a stop keeping the slick just offshore of the little rocky island. They set out buoys to mark the edges of the oil. Jonah and his crew monitored the slick from the air with his seaplane taking photos throughout the day, and with a boat taking samples of the water.

They sent divers into the water to gauge the depth of the oil disbursement. The calm seas and cold water had caused the oil to clump into millions of balls the size of marbles with the mass of it stretching three feet deep and dancing on the surface.

On the second day the water samples showed a tremendous decrease in the oxygen levels, and an increase of carbon dioxide, clear indications that the bacteria was eating the carbon in the oil and expelling it as a gas.

Using the helicopters and the canister sprayers they spread a liquid mixture of phosphorus and nitrogen to fertilize the microbes and speed up their hungry ways.

The calm weather stayed on, turning the Gulf of Alaska into a sort of tropical doldrums. By day five the slick was half the size. By day ten it was gone. What remained was a two mile wide dead zone void of oxygen and full of the oil eating microbes. Eventually the microbes sank to the bottom of the sea, and were devoured by plankton on the way down.

Scientists with the Environmental Protection Agency had been on the scene taking samples and photos of their own, and were shocked at their findings. The oil was gone. They sent robotic submersibles to the ocean floor to search for oil that may have sunk. The bottom was clean.

No one in Jonah's crew had slept more than a couple of hours a day for the past week and a half. Jonah had grounded himself from lack of sleep, and was using the helicopters for reconnaissance. His pilot was impressed.

"Nice work. That little team you put together had a great game."

Jonah nodded. It had worked. Somehow with the combination of factors all lined up in their favor it had worked. The little microbes did their job. If the current was running, and the wind was blowing, if it was raining or cloudy, or the middle of winter with no sun, then things might have been different.

It was a breakthrough of epic proportions. And soon word got out.

4.

Sheik Abdul Ali waved his visitor into the chamber. His traditional robe and headdress flowed as he waved. He was very large even by Sheik standards, weighing in at over three hundred pounds. The food and drink at the palace was endless and now with his new chef from Istanbul he was enjoying the pleasure of Eurasian cuisine again. Curses on his old chef who tried to poison him with tasteless meals meant for peasants. Now bound in chains in the dungeon beneath the palace, that nameless swine would rue the day he dared to dish up such swill.

Educated in London and New York, and now back in the Gulf, the sheik was happy and full of life and vigor, and why not?

With the price of oil at an all time high and production steady and rising, there was every reason to celebrate. And celebrate the Sheik would.

"Come, come be at ease." He motioned his visitor to sit in one of the large velvet chairs nearby. "To what do I owe this visit Dr. Moldini?"

"Thank you Sheik Abdul." The small dark Italian bowed deep to the Sheik and kissed the extended ring before sitting down.

Aldin Moldini was a chemist from a small town in Sicily. When he was only fifteen he graduated from Europe's finest University with honors. When he was twenty he patented a technique that injected microbes into oil wells that made the oil more slippery if that can be imagined. The microbes lined the walls of the porous pools of precious black liquid, and made it easier to extract. Production went up, and the cartel hired him to oversee first one facility, and eventually the whole production of oil in the country. Now in his fifties and with a younger generation of chemists and engineers running the show, Dr. Moldini was more of a consultant these days.

When the sheik was young and forced by his father to study abroad he took an interest in chemistry, but it proved to be much too difficult. The good Dr. Moldini took him under his wing and showed him some tricks to pass his courses. The sheik would never be a world class chemist, but since he was the sheik he didn't really need to be one. And yet he still had that nagging interest in chemistry, especially anything that had to do with oil. And so one of Dr. Moldini's jobs was keep him informed of any new inventions, secret or otherwise. He searched throughout the world using a network of friends and thieves and spies, and when anything of note came to the surface he went straight to the sheik.

The sheik poured a shot of whiskey in a small crystal glass, placed it on the side table next to Moldini and poured one for himself. The sheik raised his glass in a toast.

"Shucram"

"Shucram," Moldini replied and returned the toast, and then sipped at the whiskey. It burned his throat going down and he winced.

"Ah hah!," the sheik laughed and slapped him on the back. "Still the same Moldini. So what is new my friend, any new chemical breakthroughs that can help us make more money with our oil?"

Moldini was still wincing from the whiskey and the sheik became impatient. "What about the Americans and their fracking techniques? Is there anything new there? I understand there is a new method being tested to make it less expensive and less dangerous for the environment. This is one of our greatest fears of course. Our grip on world oil will be gone if they are able to extract that oil at less a price than we provide. And their reserves are huge if they can utilize that technique; I don't have to tell you that."

The sheik took another short glass of Whiskey and swirled it and watched the amber color mix with the ice before sipping on it and continuing.

"We'll have to put more pressure on our people in the Senate, and Congress and the White House using our proxies in the media. Fracking is still very dangerous to the environment, no matter what the crazy and evil and greedy oil producers in America may say. They'll ruin the land and destroy the country to get a drop of oil. That's the message we need to get across."

"It's not any new techniques of drilling or

pumping or finding oil that you need to worry about."

"Well what then?"

Moldini set his glass down and sat back in his chair. "Two months ago your highness there was an oil spill in the Prince William Sound south of Alaska. Not an especially large spill, just a little under five hundred barrels of crude. Around twenty thousand gallons or about seventy six thousand litres"

The sheik scoffed. "Dr. Moldini, I can convert barrels into gallons and liters, and also into dollars and cents. So they lost around fifty thousand dollars worth of oil. That is like a single malnourished flea on the entire herd of camels in the Gulf."

"Yes," Moldini agreed, "it was a small amount comparatively. However, it is what happened after the spill that interests me, that should interest you."

The sheik leaned forward, intrigued.

"Continue."

5.

Jonah leaned back in the seat and sighed. "I hate speeches." He was looking out the window in business class as they made their approach to La Guardia airport. The sky was grey with smog; the ground below was barren. The plane shook slightly as the flaps were lowered. "And why would anyone want to schedule a conference in New York in the middle of summer? Couldn't they schedule it for Florida, or Las Vegas?"

The man in the seat next to him chuckled. "Well hey, why not Bermuda, or Hawaii? We're still a new technology Jonah. We've got to go where the action is, where the money is. I know we've come a long ways, but there's a lot of competition, it's getting cut throat now that there's the potential for real money to be made. You see Able Cummings and his gang up in first class?"

"Yeah, I see them."

"They're spending money like drunken sailors, but it's not their money, it's from their backers who they've talked into thinking they're going to control the wonderful world of chemical spill cleanups. There's big money lining up in the pipeline so to speak, a lot of pressure is being put on the producers of oil and gas to clean up their act, the world governments are taking a harder line, legal remedies are becoming much more expensive and the producers are looking for another alternative. And we're going to provide it for them."

Ross O'Malley was a business man, self made and driven. Seventy eight years old and brought up in the serious times after world war two, he determined early on in life to succeed. And succeed he had. He started with a simple patent that he devised in college, and then built a biomedical conglomerate from the ground up, finding genius chemists and medical students in universities around the world, funding their education and research, and reaping the benefits with fourteen hundred patents and counting. Now he was entering a new field, the world of bioremediation. So late in life it gave him a spark to be doing something new and different and he was intrigued by the possibility of coming up with the new big thing.

"Jonah my boy, this is the chance of a lifetime. As a minor stockholder in this company, you stand to make a fortune by giving a little speech. Let's not even call it a speech, let's just call it a little talk between friends, and colleagues. A little chit chat."

"I don't care about making a fortune Ross; I just want to have clean water and shorelines. And I will find a way to achieve that end."

"Aw yes, the ever pragmatic scientist."

Jonah shook his head. "And I don't believe

this speech is going to make one bit of difference in the way these clowns think. Half of them are envious, and the other half want to see me fail, and not one of them will believe the results. They're scientists Ross; they don't believe anything unless they perform the tests themselves, or unless it's been proven beyond a shadow of a doubt, which takes years."

Ross just smiled. "We're not here for the scientists Jonah, we're here for the people on the sidelines who watch these conferences in the shadows, the ones who pull the levers of power and money, the ones who make the decisions on what products to use, they're the ones you'll be talking to. We are on the verge of something very big, I can feel it."

"Maybe, but what we have now is a temporary fix for a specific type of spill on the ocean. Sure it worked, and it'll work again in similar situations, but it's like a band aid when we need a full body cast. When oil gets loose it's a monster, if you don't stop it at the source of the spill it goes a little ways underground and hides."

"That's why we need to make sure our microbe is in the hands of every oil producing and remediation company in the world. Wherever there's a single drop of oil on the water they need to be certain that they can contain it and eliminate it, no matter what the financial cost it is to purchase our brand of microbe."

"It's all about the money right?"

"Money funds research Jonah. You just keep

up the research and I'll handle the rest. It was a lucky break that you were in the Gulf of Alaska when that spill happened, and now we need to capitalize on it." Ross tightened his seatbelt and closed his eyes for the landing.

It was more than a lucky break, thought Jonah. It was a gift from above. The microbe strain worked, he had proven it. In those perfect conditions they worked magnificently. However the real test lay ahead. Bioremediation of a crude oil slick on the open ocean was not done very often and for good reason. Wind and waves usually spread the slick, quickly mixing it deep into the ocean and onto the shoreline.

Once heavy oil reached the shore, or seeped into a marsh, or beach, it became much more difficult to contain and eradicate. Without a steady source of oxygen, and light, most oil eating bacteria lost their swagger so to speak. They became weak and dysfunctional. And over time the spilled oil became weathered and tough, like tar or asphalt, and there it would linger in pockets just below the surface for decades and reappear after storms or big waves. The real test was to create a strain that would devour the landlocked oil, the stuff that was buried under rock and sand. Now that would be big, thought Jonah, real big. He'd need nothing short of a miracle to figure that one out, but figure it out he would, or die trying. For what else was there in life?

Each man, woman and living creature on earth had a job to do, placed here by the almighty for a reason. His job was to clean oil, and he would damn well do that job to the best of his ability. He had royalties from his little microbe inventions to keep him financially secure for the rest of his life, but there would be no retiring for him, he made that decision long ago. He would find a problem and solve it, and when that problem was solved he'd find another until his time was up. The problem with the oil buried on shorelines and marshes was elusive, and he'd solved other problems in the meantime while keeping that one on the back burner in a big pot, not on high or low, but simmering like a great Scottish stew on a cold frosty morning.

He'd taken the problems he'd solved like the recent oil eating bug and placed it carefully into the thinking stew and kept it simmering, and adding in new spices and ingredients as they came along. There was something missing, still absent from the brew, maybe a few items that didn't even exist as yet, some engineered gene that a biologist was working on in a dark lab in the middle of nowhere that would be the key.

The wheels were lowered from the plane; he could hear the hydraulics extending the frames and then a slight bump as they locked in place. The pilot was making his final approach in a big sweeping turn. Jonah imagined himself at the wheel, man wouldn't this be a fun plane to fly, and he would take it around the world hopping from airport to airport, across the north and south poles, over every ocean and continent.

There was a bump from turbulence and the fuselage shook. A woman across the aisle gripped the seat and looked nervously towards the cockpit. Jonah winked at her and gave her a thumbs up to reassure her. "Just a little bump."

"I hate the landings," she said and tried to smile. It was a feeble attempt and fell just short of a grimace.

"Me too," Jonah lied. "I wish I was at the controls, don't you? It sure would be a lot more fun." He pretended he was driving the plane with his hands on the wheel turning it right and left.

Her smile flashed wide and genuine as she thought about that, and then a quick bump and jostle later and she was back to a grimace.

The plane landed hard bouncing on the tarmac a couple of times with that sound of screeching tires, and then the engines blasted hard in reverse to slow them down. Within moments the hurtling aircraft was taxiing smoothly down the runway and they could see the lights of the terminal to the side. The woman breathed in relief and the smile on her face did not leave for quite some time.

Jonah motioned towards the cockpit with a nod of his head and whispered to her, "Rookies."

6.

Jonah stood at the podium and looked out at the crowd. Over three hundred scientists and industry executives were seated in an auditorium in the hotel. He tapped on the microphone, and it reverberated throughout the room. Many in the audience frowned. He pulled at his beard and cleared his throat.

Alright, he thought, here goes nothing. I'll break the ice with a little joke. He leaned down towards the microphone. "Why do bacteria like nitrates so much?"

The crowd was silent, impatient.

Out in the audience Abby Campbell smiled wryly, and thought to herself. 'Because they're cheaper that the day rates.'

"Because they're cheaper than the day rates," Jonah continued out loud with a grin. A few of the people in the audience laughed but most of them kept their serious faces. Tough crowd.

Jonah's goofy grin faded and he sighed. "Well, maybe it's too early in the morning for jokes, so let's get down to business. Most of you have heard about our recent success using a genetically modified bacterial microbe to remediate an oil spill in Alaska a few weeks ago. We'll be publishing a paper in the coming months, but for now I'd like to detail some of the processes that we used with that operation. One of the challenges with the application of microbes over large areas in non-stable environments is keeping them focused in the target area, and once they are interacting with the toxic environment, to maintain and increase their ability to eradicate the toxins. We were able to fix our microbes into a liquid gel that had many of the same characteristics of the crude oil we were attempting to eliminate. It's like glue that attaches to the microbes and the oil and bonds them together. The open ocean environment that we were operating in was rather stable at the time and so the microbes and oil slick stayed relatively close together. Once the gel mixture was in place the emphasis shifted to fertilizing the microbes to increase their reproduction. And so getting back to my opening joke, as we all know, bacterial microbes utilize nitrate like a vitamin..."

Jonah talked for half an hour on the nuts and bolts of applying the oil eating bacteria to different scenarios, touching briefly on the obstacles that are encountered with transportation and application in the wild, both on land and sea.

"...and so in conclusion, whether it's a marsh or a lake, the middle of the ocean, or a field in your home town, oil spills are an ongoing problem that we'll be faced with as long as mankind has the need to transport large quantities of the toxic material. Thank you for listening"

He looked around the room, surprised that no

one had left. "Any questions?"

Abby raised her hand from the back of the room. Jonah shielded his eyes from the lights so he could see her better.

Holy cow, he thought, what a beauty. She must be a reporter or something, couldn't be a scientist. "Yes, in the back," he motioned to her and she got to her feet.

"Dr. MacLean, I know you said you'll be publishing a paper soon on your modified bacteria, but can you just give a quick recourse on the plasmid DNA restructuring, was it simultaneous or in separate steps?"

Plasmid DNA restructuring? Ok, she's no reporter, he thought. "Yes," he replied, "We'll be disclosing all that information in our paper, but I can tell you it was a simultaneous restructure utilizing many separate plasmid donors in a combined sequence."

The event organizers were coming onto the stage, and Jonah looked at his watch. "Well folks, it looks like I've used up my time for today. I'll be around if anyone has additional questions. Thanks again."

Polite applause filled the room as he stepped off the stage.

A thin balding man in a grey suit stepped to the microphone. "Thank you Dr. McLean. And now we'll have a quick fifteen minute break before our next speaker, Dr. Noel Aventine who will give a presentation of the Biology of Symbiotic Systems.

Sitting at the front of the room, Dr. Aldin Moldini turned off his mini recorder, and stood up. He was impressed with the presentation. It appeared that Jonah and his company would be increasing research towards spills that were trapped in soils and marshlands. That was a major concern with oil producing countries Middle East where the volume was so tremendous and the potential for oil leaking into the ground and winding up in the underground water table was inevitable. Water after all was more precious than oil in these countries. That is, for the common man at any rate. For the sheiks it was oil at any cost, the more they could pump produce and sell, the better off they were.

This microbe that Jonah had created was of special interest to the oil producers, and Dr. Moldini was here at the convention to find out as much as he could about it. He was sent here to spy.

As long as the microbe was used to remediate oil that was inadvertently spilled, they had no problems with it and would let it go untouched, but Aldin Moldini knew his old student too well.

He followed Jonah out to the foyer where many people had gathered around and were talking shop. Jonah was surrounded.

"Hello Jonah."

Jonah turned and his face soured a bit as he reached out his hand. "Dr. Moldini, how have you been? Still working for the enemy?"

Moldini laughed. "Now Jonah. We are

working towards the same goal, the efficient and waste proof transportation of oil from the ground to the tank."

"If that was possible, I'd be on your side. There are a few of us who would like nothing more than to eliminate the need for oil entirely. We are as you say on different sides of the fence now, you pump the oil, and I clean up the mess it makes."

The pretty woman who asked the question in the auditorium approached from the side.

"Congratulations on your recent success Dr. MacLean."

Jonah smiled as he turned and his jaw dropped a bit when he saw her. "Why thank you," he replied, "but please call me Jonah, there was a bit of luck involved. Say you look really familiar, have we met?"

"I'm sure I would have remembered." She replied.

"School, work, another exciting micro biotic convention?"

She laughed. "No I don't think so; this is the first one I've ever attended. I'm new in the field. My training was in genetics research at MIT, and I've been working with the Woods Hole Institute for the past year."

"That's where I've seen you! Well I mean I saw a picture of you getting out of a submarine with a crack across the whole windshield. The black smoker fiasco." He shook his head and whistled. "Holy cow, a close call eh?"

She blushed. That dang picture, somehow it made it into every newspaper and magazine in the world, and it wasn't a very flattering image of her climbing out the sub with a frightened look on her face, hair sticking out all over the place. "Yes, well… Anyways, I made the trip here because I wanted to meet you and talk to you face to face about your, creation. My name is Abby Campbell."

"I'm sorry, I'm being rude, have you met Dr. Aldin Moldini?"

"A pleasure," Moldini bowed deep and kissed her hand.

"He's Italian," said Jonah.

"Yes I can tell," she said still blushing.

"We worked together on a project long ago," said Jonah. "I was fresh out of college and eager for work. I was his research assistant for a year on an oil extracting microbe that made him famous, and rich."

"Well, it's nothing compared to what is happening now," said Moldini. "That was an existing microbe that we found a new use for, and I'm always grateful for your excellent research." He turned to Abby. "We found a microbe that helped thin the heavy oil at the surface of a well in order to ease in extracting the precious fluid." He turned back to Jonah. "What you are doing now Jonah is quite different, and in some ways much more sophisticated."

"There's quite a lot of work left to be done. In fact I don't know where to begin."

"I do," Abby interjected. "In fact that's why I'm here."

Jonah and Moldini looked at her with puzzled faces.

"I'd like to talk about a joint research project," she hesitated. "That is talk with you Jonah, in private if you don't mind."

Moldini smiled. "Yes, well it seems I find myself as the proverbial third wheel."

"I'm sorry Dr. Moldini," said Abby. "I didn't mean to interrupt your reunion. Jonah if it's okay we can meet whenever you have the time."

Moldini held his hand up.

"No, I think Jonah and I can meet at a later time. Oh, by the way I have a gift that you two can use right away." He reached into his coat pocket and pulled out an envelope. "It's a two hundred dollar gift certificate to the finest Italian seafood restaurant in town, Bonavelli's. I know the owners and they left this for me in my hotel. I have prior engagements and I want to make sure it's put to good use."

Jonah reached out and accepted the envelope. "Why thank you Aldin. We'll put this to good use. Now if you'll excuse me, I'll say good evening."

Moldini bowed and kissed Abby's hand again. "Oh, one more favor. Abby would you take a picture of Jonah and me with my phone?"

"Of course," Abby said and reached out for the phone.

Moldini put his arm around Jonah. "Once he was my assistant, and now he's on his way to becoming a great scientist."

Abby clicked the photo and handed the phone back to Moldini who shook Jonah's hand. "We'll be in touch my friend," and he walked away.

"What a nice man," remarked Abby.

"Yeah, a real work of art," said Jonah.

Outside the foyer, Moldini walked quickly while talking into his phone. "Yes, Bonavelli's. Tonight, be ready. I'll send you the photo in a moment."

He hung up and then texted the photo that was just taken of himself and Jonah.

7.

Bonavelli's was in the middle of the city next to a soaring hotel. Jonah waited outside in the waning dusk, the heat of the day slowly easing from the streets. He'd walked from his hotel which he estimated was over a mile away, and it felt great to be outside even in this beehive of a city. The valet station in front of the restaurant was busy shuffling cars and people.

He counted no fewer than ten runners greeting the cars, ushering the guests towards the doorway and driving off in the cars, then emerging from the corner running towards the front ready for another car. And the autos; Bentleys and Range Rovers, Lexis and Hummers, Cadillac's and Mercedes Benz. He even saw a red Ferrari, and the couple who got out of that car were super smooth, like they'd just gotten out of a spa at the Ritz, all shiny and slicked back just like their car, with that look of confidence like they could rule the world.

Wow, thought Jonah, this really must be a great restaurant, just as Moldini advertised. He felt in his pocket for the gift certificate. After all he'd been through with Moldini, and for him to accept this little crumb.

"I must be getting soft," he muttered. This is dirty money, he thought, and I wish there was a way to clean it.

About fifty feet away stood a ruffled old man wearing ruffled old clothes and panhandling. He wasn't saying anything to the people walking by; he just stood there holding his hat with both hands by his waist. He'd nod and smile as the people passed him whether they donated or not. Now and then someone would reach out and drop a coin or a bill into the hat and his smile would grow wider and he'd give his thanks.

Jonah walked over and stood near the man. "Evening sir," the old one said. His hair was silver and combed neat. His silver moustache had a tinge of black at the center as though a bit of him were holding onto his youth. The creases in his face and the wrinkles near his eyes told a tale of smiles through the years.

"Good evening to you sir," Jonah said. "Having a tough time of it are you?"

"No sir, it's all very well tonight, the air is fresh, the ground is firm, and the grace of our Lord is with us." The creases in his skin pulled together as one, and a peaceful smile filled his face. "I'd rather be working, but I'm old now and no one will hire me. Aw, but when I was young I was strong..." His eyes got misty as he looked at Jonah. "I had many fine paying jobs and I could work all day and through the night. I helped build some of the big buildings you see on this block. Lifting cement and welding beams, working high in the air." He gazed up at the skyscrapers around them. "And then I'd work inside the hotels when they were finished being built. I was a mason and a chef, a bricklayer and a butler, and now I'm just an old man standing here with my memories."

"You see that restaurant?" asked Jonah.

"Oh yes," said the old man. "You'll have a fine meal in there young sir, that is for certain."

"I want you to take this gift certificate," Jonah reached into his coat pocket and took out the envelope. "And go have a nice meal, or two in there."

The old man slowly shook his head. "Thank you sir, but they'll never let me in the door." He looked down at his clothes. "I wouldn't fit in."

Jonah frowned. "Yeah I suppose you're right. I don't fit in either." Then his eyes brightened, and he snapped his fingers. "Hey I'll bet they have take out."

The old man's eyes brightened in return and a smile reappeared. "You know, I'll bet they do."

Jonah pushed the envelope into the old man's hand and clapped him on the back. "C'mon, I'll go with you."

They walked together down the sidewalk towards the restaurant, like two bookends of life itself. The car valets nodded in acknowledgement as they approached. They knew the old man; he was a regular on the block and never made any trouble.

Jonah held the old man back with gentle touch on his elbow. "Let's wait a moment. I'm expecting someone."

As if on cue a taxi pulled up to the curb and out stepped the prettiest girl in the city. Her long tan legs rose up into a black velvet dress meeting her long flowing brown hair and soft shoulders, ruby red lips spread in a lovely smile as she paid the cab driver. All the men from the cab driver to the valets, to the doorman and Johan and the old man looked stunned as she got out of the cab. They all stopped what they were doing as though hypnotized. A car going by honked and someone whistled out the window.

"Hello," she said to Jonah. "I hope you haven't been waiting too long."

"Uh, no, you look uh…"

"Very beautiful miss," the old man filled in as he nodded in the affirmative.

Abby's cheeks blushed. "Well, Dr. Moldini did say it was the best restaurant in the city, I didn't know what to wear."

Jonah smiled, "You look perfect. I'd like you to meet a friend of mine," and he turned towards the old man.

"Sam Roubelli Miss," the old man bowed and fairly creaked as he did so.

"Pleased to meet you," Abby extended her hand and the old man thought briefly to kiss it as a knight of yore, but then nodded meekly.

"The pleasure is mine."

Jonah noted the exchange with satisfaction. "Alright then," he declared. "Let's see if this place can live up to the hype."

They strolled past the valets who all nodded in acknowledgement. The doorman beamed as they approached.

"Good evening folks, do you have reservations?

"Evening," said Jonah. "Yes, a table for two, MacLean. Do you have an area in the restaurant where Mr. Roubelli here can order some take out?"

The doorman started to wince as he looked at the old man, but then the overwhelming presence of Abby's beauty pulled him back. "Why yes sir, we have an alcove where he can order take out and wait, if that would be okay" He smiled at Abby.

Jonah put a folded twenty into the doorman's hand as the silver doors were opened for them and they entered an Italian village and the aroma of garlic butter, and fresh bread, and pasta wafted through the room. A piano and violin were playing in the far corner while a waiter torched a peach flambé to the delight of the patrons at the surrounding tables.

A young hostess greeted them, and the doorman introduced them to her.

"The MacLean party. And this is Mr. Roubelli who will be ordering some food to go."

"Wonderful," she smiled, as she gestured to the large alcove with leather chairs to the side.

"Mr. Roubelli we have a comfortable room where you can take a look at the menu, and I'll be back to take your order."

"Thank you." The old man reached out and grasped Jonah's hand. "God bless you young man."

"You take care of yourself Mr. Roubelli, and perhaps we'll meet again."

The old man shuffled off into the alcove and settled into a leather chair with a sigh.

Abby and Jonah followed the hostess into the room. The place was packed, every table but one was full. They wound their way towards the back towards a table near the piano, where a team of waiters were busy smoothing out a new white table cloth and arranging the plates and silverware. By the time they reached the table it was ready. They settled in and ordered cocktails, Abby a glass of Chardonnay, and Jonah a beer on tap. They toasted with a clink of glasses.

"Well this is nice," she said. "I wanted to talk to you about your research, but I never expected to meet in a place like this. I feel like we're actually in Italy."

"Yes, it was very nice of Dr. Moldini to offer this, very nice indeed."

She pushed her wine glass to the side and leaned towards him. "I have so many questions to ask you…"

Jonah put his index finger to his lips in the universal 'quiet' sign and she stopped mid sentence with a puzzled look.

He was studying the flower vase on the edge of the table with narrowed eyes. He pulled a small Swiss army knife from his pocket and used the little scissors to snip a yellow flower from its stem. He held it closer for her to see the little microphone the size of an ant, and then he dipped it upside down into his water glass and tossed it under the table and crushed it with his heel, grinding it to a pulp.

"Was that what I think it was?"

"It was a bug."

"I know it was a bug," she whispered looking around. "But was it a 'bug'? "

"It was a microphone that looked like a bug."

She leaned over the table. "Why would someone put a microphone in a flower vase?"

"I've got an old saying, 'Always look a gift horse in the mouth'."

"Holy cow, can't you guys ever get your sayings right?"

"What?"

"Isn't it the other way around, as in 'never' look a gift horse in the mouth?"

"Not this time."

"Wait, are you saying Dr. Moldini set this up with that gift certificate?"

"Isn't it obvious?"

"How do you know that microphone, if it even was a microphone, was put there for you?"

"Oh it was a microphone alright. And you are correct, being a scientist we need absolute proof, we can't just assume anything." He frowned. "But I know Moldini."

"We're at an Italian restaurant in the city. It could have been planted to eavesdrop on a mob boss for all we know."

"A mob boss? Now that's farfetched."

"But Dr. Moldini? That nice old man?"

"That nice old man works for some of the most ruthless people in the world. There's ninety eight billion barrels of oil under the sand in a tiny corner of the Persian Gulf. At today's price that's around ten trillion dollars. With that much money at stake do you think they play nice? They'll do anything to get an edge. And they're not the only ones, they're everywhere. Where there's money, there's power, and where there's money and power there's corruption and greed. Don't get me started."

Jonah scanned the room. Someone here or very close by was monitoring the microphone that lay crushed under the table. Most likely they had a backup plan, or more devices planted. He reached into his wallet and pulled out a twenty and slid it under his beer mug.

"Let's go find another restaurant."

She didn't know him well at all, but could see the concern on his face. "Well alright, if you insist."

They walked out into the crisp night air. The city was bustling. Down the block they saw a raucous pizzeria sports bar combo, with live rock music blasting out the doors.

He pointed towards it. "How about that place?"

"It's fine with me, but I may be a little overdressed."

"Naw, you're fine."

They walked through the double doors into controlled mayhem. A four piece rock band was belting out southern rock tunes, while baseball, football, golf, wrestling and monster truck racing played on giant flat screen TV's around the room. The floor was covered in sawdust and the aroma of pizza and beer filled the air along with loud voices and laughter. Hooters style waitresses waded through the crowd carrying mugs and pitchers. They found an empty table in the corner and sat down. An especially endowed waitress came over and greeted them with a big smile.

"Hi folks, just the two of you?"

"Yep," said Jonah, trying not to stare. "Nice place you have here."

"Oh this is a slow night. You should see it when we have Monday night football, just crazy. Would you something to drink while you look at the menu?"

Jonah shook his head. "Sure, I'll just take a beer. What about you Abby?"

"A beer's fine with me too."

"I thought you shouldn't mix beer and wine."

"We left so quickly I didn't have a chance to take a sip."

"Alright, well how about a pitcher? Light?

"Aw heck, Jonah, a girl has to live it up once in a while. Make it regular."

His brow lifted in appreciation.

The waitress smiled at her and nodded, "You go girl. By the way, love the dress." And she strutted off to the bar.

"Wow, I'm impressed, a woman scientist who drinks beer. You don't see that every day," said Jonah.

"I grew up on a cattle ranch. My Dad took me everywhere and taught me everything he knew about raising cattle and raising a little hell now and then. I was an only child, and I think deep down he wanted a son and so he taught me to kick butt, roping steers, and riding the range. It's pretty funny, I remember when I was sixteen and had a date to the prom, I came out of my room with a pink frilly dress and a little tear rolled down the corner of his eye. He hugged me and told me how pretty I looked, but I couldn't tell if it was a tear of joy, or despair. So anyways, the next day I got up before dawn, saddled up the horses and asked him if we could go rope some cows. He got a big goofy grin like a kid and I knew everything was going to be okay with us."

"So you didn't follow in his footsteps and stay in the family business?"

"No, I turned into an egghead pretty quick." She laughed. "When I was in Junior High I bought a microscope with my allowance, and started looking at everything I could find with the highest magnification I could get my hands on.

Everything from the farm, bull hairs, chicken feathers, dirt, you name it. Then I started growing cultures with the butt nastiest stuff I could find, and believe me, on a cattle ranch there is some really disgusting material to use as a base."

"So what's this about a joint venture Abby, why would you want to collaborate with me, I'm just a small time geneticist."

"I've read about your work, and your lab set up.

"There's plenty of bigger labs with more money, more equipment. Besides, aren't you working with the Woods Hole Institute?"

She got a sheepish look on her face. "They fired me."

"What?"

"Well, I sort of broke their submarine. It cost two million to repair; they had to dry dock it for three months while they fabricated a new borosilicate dome. They lost a whole summer of research. The head of the science department had to scrub his big mission as well as a whole bunch of other missions that were lined up. Time is of the essence with research, and a rival Institute picked them up."

"Ouch."

"There were a lot of angry people I'll tell you. They lost a lot of money in funding and needed a scapegoat and boy I was it."

"Sorry. Have you tried other universities, institutes?"

"Just about every one of them with any weight. I think I've been blacklisted."

"Well, I'm really flattered Abby, I don't know what to say, but I've always been a one man band except for when I was young and just getting started."

"I won't pull a Moldini on you."

"It's not that, it's just that I have my own method, my own work schedule, I guess I'm kind of a loner."

The waitress settled the pitcher on the table and placed two frosted glasses in front of them.

"Give us a minute and we'll look over the menu," said Jonah and he filled the mugs.

"To science," he said.

She clinked his glass. "To science."

"Do you remember the first time you extracted DNA?" asked Jonah.

She was taking a drink when he asked the question and she almost choked.

"Oh yeah, I remember like it was yesterday. I was about ten years old." She laughed, "I got in so much trouble. It seems pretty funny now, but at the time it was high drama. I was only in sixth grade but I was getting seriously into science, and so I got some books from the library and found an easy method, and did the experiment in our kitchen while my parents were working outside on the farm. I took some chicken eggs, mixed them in the blender with salt, then poured that into Mom's measuring cup, added some dish detergent and mixed it up, then added some meat tenderizer for the enzymes to cut the protein from the DNA, then poured some rubbing alcohol down the side of the cup to precipitate the strands of DNA, collected the long white strands with a straw and put them into a glass jar with alcohol. When my parents came home and I showed them what I'd done, they nearly had a heart attack."

"They didn't like it huh?"

"Oh my God, they were furious, mostly because they didn't understand what it was. They reacted like they'd caught me doing drugs or something. To them I was messing with nature, and since I was so young they were a little scared. I had to explain everything to them with the books and a chalkboard."

"Like you were a teacher."

"Ten years old, teaching my parents about cell microbiology. After a while they calmed down. My Dad told me, 'Just don't be mixing none of that chicken DNA with no cow DNA. I don't want to open the barn door one day and have the cows fly away.' I guess from that day on they realized I wasn't exactly a normal kid. So what about you? When did you crack open your first DNA?"

"You beat me by a few years on that one. I was twelve, just got back from Alaska, cleaning the Exxon Valdez spill with my Dad and I was suddenly on a mission. I probably read the same book that you did on extracting DNA, but I used some fresh salmon. It was weird; I remember being a little bit freaked out when I saw those long strands of DNA floating in the alcohol. And then I injected it into one of my goldfish, I thought I could get it to turn into a salmon overnight. It died. My Dad found out and called me his little mad scientist, but warned me not to do something like again."

"And yet here you are," she said.

"Still a rebel."

The waitress came back to their table. "Ready to order?"

"Hmm," Jonah looked at Abby. "How about a big 'ol pizza with the works. Garlic, anchovies, olives, peppers, mushrooms…"

"And shrimp," Abby finished for him.

"No shrimp." Jonah shook his head.

"No shrimp?" She asked puzzled.

"Nope."

"Alright, no shrimp," she agreed with a frown.

"It'll be about twenty five minutes, good choice!" exclaimed the waitress as she walked to the kitchen.

Jonah filled their glasses again and they toasted for the third time that night.

"To your health," he pledged.

"To health," she agreed as the mugs clinked together. "You don't like shrimp, but you do like anchovies?"

"Well, ever since the BP oil spill in the Gulf of Mexico I've laid off the shrimp unless I know exactly where it's from. The anchovies swim in the upper layer of ocean, shrimp crawl around in the muck and leftover oil residue."

"Is it still a problem, the oil spill?"

"I'll give it another twenty years."

"Twenty years… I thought it was taken care of."

"Well you see the oil is not really gone, it just seeped into the mud at the bottom of the ocean. It just looks like it's gone, but it's everywhere down there and covers a vast area, probably around five hundred square miles. Right there in the prime shrimping zone. It think most of the shrimp fishermen avoid that area, but who knows? And it really sucks because I like to eat shrimp."

"You don't like crude oil do you?"

"I like clean air and water."

"Which brings us to your adventure up north, and the spill in the Prince William Sound. Did you take core samples of the bottom?" "We did."

"And?"

"Well, there was a trace of hydrocarbon molecules from the spill but in such a minute amount that it almost could have been background or natural pollution."

"It sounds like a tremendous breakthrough. I can't wait to read the paper."

"It's just a small step forward. My ultimate goal is to eliminate the need for oil in the first place. There has to be another way around this problem, this energy problem besides pumping the damn oil out of the ground and polluting the hell out of our little planet. I think it's meant to stay where it's at, deep underground. I've seen the devastation when it gets loose and it's ugly and doesn't go away once it gets into the soil. We should be smarter than this. If we can put a man on the moon we should be able to invent an alternate energy."

"Like what?"

"I don't know, like oil on demand, synthetic, mixed on the spot, or hydrogen engines using water as the main component."

"Now you're just dreaming."

"Hey a guy's got to dream. But right now my focus is on creating a form of bacteria that can go underground and eat the oil that seeps into the soil after a spill. That's a problem I should be able to fix in the near future. I'm working on it. I'm getting close, but I'm missing something."

"What if you could get rid of all the oil in world, you know eat all the oil" she asked.

"In the world?"

"In the whole dang world."

"In a heartbeat."

"Are you kidding me? We'd be back at the days of riding around in horse and buggies, coal and steam trains."

"That's not such a bad thing, but it wouldn't happen."

"Why?"

"We'd get another energy source. About five minutes after the last drop of oil was gone. The research and development would put the

Manhattan project to shame. Heck, they probably already the alternative figured out, but locked up in a vault somewhere."

"Conspiracy theorist?"

"Just a theory, you see there's no money in it, no control, and no monopoly. It's something so plentiful and easy to use that with the right tool or engine, the average Joe would be independent. And if someone hasn't already figured it out, I will."

"You seem pretty confident."

He winked at her. "A guys gotta be confident."

"So you'd eat all the oil if you could."

He snapped his fingers. "Like that."

She topped off his mug and leaned forward. "All dreaming aside and getting back to your real life problem of developing a microbe that can survive and thrive and eat all the oil down to, what? Ten feet?"

"At least a hundred."

"Why so deep?"

"Why not? I mean why take a chance on leaving that stuff anywhere near the surface so it can be exposed with some natural event. In fact why not make a microbe that can go deeper than a hundred feet, why not a thousand, five thousand? I think if we can devise something that will go even twenty feet underground and thrive; we can tweak it to go a thousand.

"I think I can help."

"How?"

"You know the bacteria I was collecting with the submarine, around the vents at the bottom of the ocean."

"I'm listening."

"They thrive under high pressure, no light, no oxygen. There's something in that DNA that could be the key to what you need. We just need to dig into it and find out."

"Can you get the samples? It doesn't sound like they're very fond of you over at the institute."

"I lost my job." And then she smiled slyly. "But I kept my samples. They were so angry about the sub that they forgot to ask about them. I call it severance pay." She pulled out a small pad of paper and pen and began drawing lines and squares, diagrams of DNA. "You need to develop an oil eating bacteria that can live underground without the normal environment of oxygen and light for synthesis. I think I found your answer."

He leaned forward and squinted at the drawing on the table.

"I have a couple of microbes that need neither light nor oxygen to thrive, and I think I've isolated a couple of the genes that sets them apart from other bacteria." She drew a line connecting two helix columns and pointed to them. "Here and here. I propose that we work together to combine our little creatures and create a super bug that can thrive and eat all the oil that it's little heart desires, all the way to the center of the earth if it wants to."

He pulled the pad of paper and rotated it so he could see the lines clearly. "These are the genes?"

She blushed as she nodded. "Sorry it's a rough sketch."

He sat silent for a moment, studying the paper, and then scrunched his eyes and tapped his chin for a few minutes. Finally after what seemed like an eternity to her, he said, "Alright, we'll do it, but on one condition. I call the shots."

She hesitated, but it was the only chance she had. "Deal. Maybe we'll create a monster bacteria that once it starts going, it just keeps on chomping right on down through the earth and eats all the oil."

"Wouldn't that be something," he mused.

The waitress set a steaming hot pizza in the middle of the table and Jonah lifted his glass towards Abby.

"Enough business talk. It's a done deal, we'll catch the first flight back to Seattle and get to work. But for now, let's eat…" Their beer mugs clinked and he continued, "…partner."

"There's just one little thing," she said.

"What's that?"

"Can we take the train instead?"

"That'll take two days.

"Actually three days," she admitted sheepishly, "I already looked into it. That's how I got here actually."

'You're afraid of flying?"

"Let's just say I avoid it."

He studied her. It was one thing to love to fly as he did, loved to actually fly the plane, but he wasn't so thrilled about being a passenger either, and so he could relate in a way, and he was never one to play down someone's fears, real or imagined since he wasn't in their shoes. She hadn't said she was afraid of flying per se, but what else could it be?

"This is really important to you?"

"I can meet you there. I don't want you to suffer on my account."

He thought again. Three days stuck on a train. And then he remembered.

"You know, I have taken a train ride across the country before. I was little, probably around eight or nine, with my Dad, and we went from Boston to Seattle. We went through the northwest stopping at a couple of little towns along the way for a day of fishing, wherever there was a stream or lake nearby we'd hop off and spend the day and the night, and then we would get back on and keep on our merry way. It was a weeklong trip, if I remember correctly. I'd forgotten all about it till now."

"We can make it a working trip."

Jonah put the pad of paper on the side and they clinked their mugs, sealing the deal.

A few tables away in an upper alcove sat a middle aged man with shaded eyeglasses and a balding forehead. He was facing down towards Jonah and Abby, and was reading a newspaper. He had a plate of nachos and a soda, and seemed to be enjoying himself, oblivious to his surroundings. Sitting on the table in front of him was what looked like a mini boom box radio, but was in fact a video and audio recorder with a telescopic HD lens and a parabolic microphone. He had a little earphone in one ear to monitor the audio and watched the video signal on a little monitor in one of his eyeglasses. The waitress came over to check on him.

"Would you like another soda sir?"

"I'm still working on this one thanks."

She motioned to his earphone. "Don't you like the band?"

"They're fine. I'm listening to them with one ear, and a baseball game with my other."

"Oh."

When Jonah put the paper pad away and clinked the mug with Abby, the middle aged man put a wad of bills on the table, picked up the boom box and walked past the waitress and out the door without saying another word. The waitress looked at him as he departed with a frown on her face. "Now, I wonder what got into him."

8.

Moldini sat at a desk in his suite, and tapped a pencil against the marble surface. The middle aged man from the pizza restaurant was sitting on the other side of the table. His name was Monroe and he was fifty eight years old and retired from the CIA. He was a trained specialist in surveillance with thirty years in the service, but when the new administration came to Washington cuts were made, and he was one of them. Retired, sure, forced retirement, and at fifty eight years old with a pension that barely paid the bills he was out on the streets.

He could go to work as store security at one of the malls, be a mall cop, or a bank guard, but that seemed to be a little too boring after what he'd been through with the agency. One day while relaxing at the park in the center of the city, watching the pigeons and wondering where all the time had gone another forced retiree sat down next to him and told him some people wanted to hire him. So he did what a lot of ex-CIA agents do after forced retirement, went to work in industrial espionage. R&D the old fashioned way. Research and development was way more expensive than letting the other guy figure a solution to a problem, and just stealing the invention. And the pay for doing the stealing was a lot more than what the CIA had been paying. Sometimes a guy had to look out for number one. He finished with his debriefing to Moldini.

"... and after he found the microphone and crushed it under the table, they left the restaurant," said Monroe.

Moldini stopped tapping the pencil and broke it in half. His face calm, but inside was turmoil, "Go on," he said between clenched teeth.

Monroe continued. "I followed them to a pizza parlor. It was very loud, much too loud for the mini dish microphone to pick up much of their conversation, but I think we got enough. I can run it through the audio filter program and it might help."

He took a computer disc from his front pocket and slid it across the marble table. "The camera in the boom box worked like a charm. I got some screen grabs from the video, you can see for yourself."

Moldini slid the disc into a laptop on the desk and clicked an icon on the screen. An amateur looking movie played on the computer screen. It was inside the pizza restaurant. He scrolled on the mouse and zoomed into the frame, and froze the image. The pad of paper filled the screen and the scribbled DNA helix although a little fuzzy with the magnification was clear as day to Dr. Moldini.

"Well, well, well," he murmured, "what do we have here? Bacterial DNA."

The audio was horrendous, and loud crowd noises filled the speakers.

"These Americans and their sports bars. Barbaric." Moldini clicked another icon and an audio filter tool popped up on the screen. Using the volume control, he isolated the voices that he wanted to hear and muted all the background noise. It was barely audible and he turned the volume up as far as it would go. He listened to the beginning of their meeting and then he leaned towards the speakers as he heard Abby's voice, "...create a super bug that can thrive and eat all the oil that its little heart desires, all the way to the center of the earth..."

Moldini picked up another pencil and sharpened it carefully, and then tapped on the computer keyboard to access the internet. Using map search he found O'Malley Bioremedial in Seattle and looked at the satellite image. Their research building was located in an industrial area south of the main city center near the freeway. There were no apartment buildings nearby.

"You'll need to find an office space nearby to rent," said Moldini. "One that is close to their research facility. Security will probably be very high in their building. Do whatever you can to gain access. I must know what they are working on."

"I'll need extra funds," said Monroe. "I may have to use a fly on the wall transmitter. They cost a hundred grand."

"You have access to one of those?" asked Moldini, suddenly impressed.

"I know a guy," was all Monroe offered. The fly on the wall was a new bug that actually looked like a bug. A miniature remote controlled fly with a microphone and transmitter. Super top secret, and in fact some people laughed it off as impossible and a hoax.

"Very well, get two" said Modini. "You'll find an extra two hundred thousand in your account. Leave tonight, and do not fail."

Monroe got up without another word and left the suite.

Moldini turned back to the computer screen and looked carefully at the pad of paper with the bacteria DNA. He played the audio over and over again. "create a super bug that can thrive and eat all the oil… eat all the oil… eat all the oil"

9.

They boarded the Amtrak train at Penn Central station at ten fifty AM on a Friday morning. It was scheduled to route through Chicago and would arrive in Seattle at ten twenty five AM on Monday morning, a seventy four hour and thirty minute trip.

Jonah bought them a 'Viewliner Roomette' that was a private room with a table in between two big seats and a drop down bunk bed, but they spent most of their time in the observation car, with the big windows and comfy seats.

They decided to make it a working trip and linked their laptops and ran sample DNA splices using the schematic graphics of the different bacteria, and over the long course of the day came up one hundred and fifty different scenarios that they felt they could start with. Then they watched a movie at the coach car, ate dinner, and went to sleep.

The next day was much of the same, breakfast at the coach car, running splicing scenarios, planning out the enzymes mixtures to cut the DNA, lunch in the coach car, watch a movie, eat dinner and sleep. By Sunday afternoon Jonah had had enough. They were passing through Colorado and right through the center of the Rocky

Mountains. Through the window he could see rivers and streams every few miles, streams that he was certain were filled with trout.

"I've got to get off this bus," he said.

"It's a train."

"Same difference."

"What's wrong."

"Cabin fever."

"On a train?"

"It's like a cabin on wheels. What do you say we take a break, get off for a while and stretch our legs."

"Can we do that?"

"I don't see why not. We'll get off at the next stop that looks good, go fishing, spend the night, and get back on the train the next day."

"Fishing?"

"I like to fish."

He went to have a talk with the valet.

"How long have you worked on this train?"

"Twenty five years sir."

"That's good, so you know your way around this train."

"Yes sir."

"We want to get off at the next town."

"For good?"

"No, I just want to stretch my legs for a day and get back on tomorrow, is that possible?"

"So you want to get off, and get back on the next day and continue on to your original destination?"

"Yeah, that's what I want to do, is it possible?"

"Yes sir, but there's a charge."

"How much?"

"One hundred dollars sir."

"Per ticket?"

"Yes sir."

"That's highway robbery."

"I know sir, I'm sorry about that."

"It's not your fault. Has anyone else ever asked you for this, what I mean to say is does anyone else ever want to just get off the train for a while on these cross country trips."

The ticket agent laughed. "I do sir."

Jonah grinned. "Funny, I mean the passengers."

"No sir, they usually just settle in and take it."

"They just take it huh?"

"Yes sir. But every now and then when the scenery is extra nice and the day is sunny, folks just want to stop for awhile and walk around in it. They tell me that when we get to talking. I wish I could go out and walk around in that field of flowers, or I wish I could climb that mountain, they tell me. They don't usually say they want to get off when it's cold and rainy or freezing snow."

"I want to get off the train and go fishing."

The ticket agent smiled wide. "Yeah, you got it, that's another thing they tell sometimes, I want to just get off this train and go fishing in that stream."

"No, I mean that's what I really want to do," said Jonah. "Do you have a list of stops up ahead?"

"Yes sir," said the ticket agent and handed him a map with little dots on it.

"Where are we at now?"

"Right here sir," he pointed to a little blue dot. "We just passed through Grand Rapids, Colorado."

"Nice country here."

"Yes sir, the good old Rocky Mountains. God sure put his mark on this place."

"So the next stop is Green River, Utah?"

"Yes sir, tiny little town, just a scrap of a town, and you know the river next to it?

"Yeah?"

"It really is the prettiest green you've ever seen."

Jonah went back to where Abby was sitting in the observation car.

"What'd you find out?" she asked him.

"It's a hundred bucks per ticket to get off and back on."

"Ouch."

He frowned at her. "Worth it." He grabbed his laptop and searched the internet. "There's a little town about a hundred miles down the track, goes by the name of Green River."

"Let me guess," she asked. "There's a green river nearby."

"Prettiest green you've ever seen," he said with a grin. On his computer screen popped up a video of the fast moving shallow river, rugged mountains in the distance, and two fishermen in waders, one of whom was fighting a fish. The title of the video was 'Fishing in Green River Utah'. "Bingo," said Jonah.

An hour later they were standing on the platform of the little town watching the train leave without them.

"We have about four more hours of sunlight to find a place to stay and then get to that river," said Jonah.

The Rocky Mountains towered all around them, and to the west the sun was getting low on the horizon. Off in the distance to the north they could see the glint from the water on the river. It was four thirty in the afternoon, and they walked to the taxi stand by the road where one lone taxi was waiting, the driver listening to a country station on the radio.

He saw them approaching with their suitcases and jumped out to help them. Tall blond and clean cut he carefully placed their bags in the trunk and held the rear door for them.

The cab although pretty old was spotless and shiny.

"Names Hiram folks, welcome to Green River, where 'bouts can I take you?"

"I'm Jonah, and this is Abby, pleased to meet you Hiram, got any hotels here?" asked Jonah as they sat in the car.

"Plenty," said Hiram, and then beamed, "but one I'd especially recommend is run by my aunt

Judy down by the library. Clean as a whistle, and comes with home cooked meals and laundry."

"Sounds great by me," he looked at Abby and she shrugged and nodded. "Let's go."

While they were driving through the town Abby noticed that everyone waved at Hiram as they passed, and Hiram waved back. In fact everyone who was driving waved at everyone else who drove past them.

"This has to be the friendliest town I've ever seen," said Abby.

"Yes ma'am, we're all friends and neighbors and relatives for the most part, so might as well say hello whenever you get the chance, even if it's just a wave."

Jonah had other things on his mind.

"So Hiram, you lived here for awhile have you?"

"All my life."

"Got any good fishing nearby."

Boy did that ever push a button, and Hiram became animated.

"Is there any good fishing?" he bellowed and just about jumped through the roof. He calmed down and got back to the business of driving after he almost ran a car off the road in his exuberance. "So you do a little fishing do you?" he asked while looking in the rear view mirror.

"I've been known to do a smidgen of it," said Jonah.

"Well okay, as soon as you get settled at the hotel, I'll take you to one of my best spots and we'll see what you got."

"Alright," said Jonah and slapped Abby's leg.

The hotel turned out to be a giant colonial house in the middle of town that was converted into an overnighter that catered to transient accommodations as well as a few full time guests that were in reality family members with nowhere else to go. It was painted bright white and had a big front lawn and a porch that could host a convention with swinging benches and lounge chairs.

"My great great granddad built the house in eighteen fifty nine," said Hiram proudly as they pulled up to the curb. He had fifteen kids so he needed a big house. There's twenty two bedrooms, a big kitchen and dining and two living rooms. Aunt Judy can sit thirty folks at a time for meals, and we had seventy five for Thanksgiving last year."

"I have to see that kitchen," said Abby.

Hiram carried their bags into the house and set them down next to a big desk by the front door, and he rang the little bell by the phone.

"She could be anywhere in the house," explained Hiram, "cleaning or cooking or fixing, so if you ever need her, just ring the bell."

A thin strong looking woman in her mid fifties came out of the back wearing an apron and fixing her hair as she walked.

"Why good afternoon folks," she said and smiled. "I was back in the kitchen getting dinner ready. You can call me aunt Judy," she said and extended her hand.

"They came off the afternoon train Aunty," said Hiram.

"Do tell, and you're staying the night?"

"Just one night Aunt Judy," said Jonah. "Tomorrow we'll continue on the train to Seattle."

"Just one night? Well, blessed heaven we're glad to have you. Come right on over and sign our registrar please, and we'll get you settled." She walked behind the desk and produced a large leather binder and a pen.

Aunt Judy was studying Abby and Jonah's left hands, looking for a ring. "Are you married?" she asked.

Abby blushed, and answered. "No."

"That will be two rooms then," said Aunt Judy without missing a beat. "I have one on the top floor and one on the bottom."

"And the barbed wire fence goes across the stairway at midnight," joked Hiram, and then his smile faded as Aunt Judy gave him a look.

"Dinner is at seven thirty sharp, it's included in the price, so don't be late, tonight we have fried chicken, mashed potatoes and gravy, corn on the cob, salad, fresh rolls and two kinds of pie, apple and blueberry."

"What's the price for the night?" asked Jonah.

"Eight five per room."

"Sounds great," said Jonah. "Do you take plastic?" as he pulled out a credit card.

She half frowned. "Well of course we do young man, this is a modern hotel."

Aunt Judy took Abby to her room on the top floor while Hiram showed Jonah his room down a long hallway from the living room.

"I think I'll need a map to find my way back," said Jonah.

"Just follow your nose," said Hiram. "The kitchen is that a way."

Jonah sniffed the air and nodded. Aunt Judy was making dinner all right; the smell of fresh country baking was certainly in the air.

"How many pies is she making?"

"At least a dozen," said Hiram. "She's a prideful woman, doesn't want anyone to miss out on a slice of pie after dinner. You probably don't know this but she is the perpetual champion blueberry pie maker at the county fair every year."

"Good old Aunt Judy," said Jonah.

"We better get goin' if we're gonna get some fishing in before supper," said Hiram.

Abby waited for Jonah on the porch and read from her book while sitting on one of the porch swings. When he came out of the front door she laughed and then stifled it with her hand to her mouth but the mirth still shone from her eyes. He was carrying two fishing poles and wearing a wide brimmed hat with fishing lures stuck all over it, and his khaki jacket with about fifty pockets also had a bunch of feathered lures stuck here and there.

"What," he said, "aint you never seen a real fisherman?"

"Did you bring all that gear with you?"

"Hey, a guy has got to be prepared. I always pack my gear; you never know when you'll come across a fishing hole."

And then Hiram came out the door and she nearly fell off the chair. If Jonah was a real fisherman, then Hiram was the king daddy of all fishermen for stuck all over his hat and his jacket with fifty pockets were over a hundred feathered lures.

It turned out that Hiram was one of the family members who lived at the house full time and had all his fishing gear ready to go at a moment's notice.

Jonah looked at him with appreciation and motioned at all the hardware hanging from his clothing. "Now see Abby, that's what I'm talking about!"

Abby just shook her and muttered. "Oh brother."

Hiram took them in his taxi through the town while waving a hundred times on the way, and turned off on a side road by an old gas station and rumbled down a dirt road for a few miles, and they came to the river and a clearing with fresh mowed grass and a freshly painted picnic table under some apple trees.

"I keep this place all nice," he beamed. "It's kind of like my own little park, but anyone is free to use it."

"Awesome," said Jonah as he stood by the car and watched the water flowing by. He turned to Abby, "Want to give it try? I brought two poles."

"I can tie on a hook," she replied. "But I'll just read my book if that's okay."

"Suit yourself." Jonah was all smiles as he headed down to the river and tied on a lure from his hat and started fly fishing, bringing the long arc of line over his head and then teasing the water with the lure giving out more line every time until he finally laid the lure gently on the water thirty feet away and it floated there, and he gave out line as it drifted with the current, and then he reeled the line in and started the dance again.

Abby watched him while trying to read her book, but he was intriguing and she couldn't look away. He looked ridiculous in the hat and jacket, but now sort of rugged and in control.

She'd had boyfriends before but they all turned out to be jerks with good looks but with no ambition or brains. Jonah seemed to have all three qualities and then some. Plus he had a good sense of humor and liked to joke around a lot. She felt comfortable around him.

Finally she put the book away and just watched him and Hiram work the bank of the river. Hiram struck first, the pole bent in half as he fought the fish towards shore, and then Jonah's reel sang and spun as a fish hit his lure. She cheered them on from the table, and when they finally landed their fish they walked close to each other to compare sizes. Typical men, thought Abby.

"It's a tie," sighed Jonah in disappointment, as they unhooked their fish and released them back into the river.

Hiram looked at his watch. "We better get going Jonah; Aunt Judy doesn't like it when folks are late for dinner."

Later that night as they were crowded around the dinner table, and all the guests were talking excitedly as Aunt Judy brought out the food, she admonished them to wait until they had said the Lord's Prayer.

"Let's all join hands," she instructed, and led them. "Our Father who art in Heaven, hallowed be thy name, thy Kingdom come thy will be done on Earth as it is in Heaven, and forgive us our trespasses as we forgive those who trespass against us, and lead us not into temptation but deliver us from evil. Amen."

Jonah was holding Abby's hand, and he noticed that she was the only one who didn't join in saying the prayer out loud. Luckily Aunt Judy didn't notice he thought, or Abby might have gone hungry that night, modern hotel be damned.

Later that night after dinner, the new guests found out that there was not a single television in the house, but there was a rousing hour of bingo before quiet time and reading.

The next day Hiram took them to the fishing hole again and Abby and Jonah stayed most of the day, fishing and reading in the shade of the apple trees by the side of river. Aunt Judy had made a picnic basket lunch for them and bid them farewell, and scolded them to get married soon and come back to visit with a big family in tow.

Before they knew it their little vacation was over, Hiram had delivered them back to the train station and they were settled into the viewing car watching Green River, Utah fade into the distance down the long line of railroad track.

10.

O'Malley Bioremedial was headquartered in the Industrial District East that was located five miles straight south of the city center of Seattle. Jonah joined the company straight out of college. At the top of his class at Stanford, he had been offered a lot of other positions but he chose O'Malley primarily for the location. The Puget Sound waterway was a mile to the west, and the Boeing county airport was two miles to the east, which meant that he could hop on his boat or his plane within minutes and get out to the wilderness.

The building was a converted warehouse that housed a research lab and production facility. It was built from concrete and hermitically sealed. It was originally constructed by an aircraft parts manufacturer that provided electronic parts for Boeing before that company downsized its operations. Barbed wire fencing surrounded the facility and an armed guard manned the gate. Community concerns about a bacteria production plant so close to the city were allayed by the security and airtight construction of the facility.

Jonah pulled up to the gate in his old Range Rover, the all terrain vehicle was a little rusty around the edges and coughed on the hills but he liked the old car and it fit his personality.

The guard on duty was obviously an ex soldier with a sculpted jaw rigid frame, and crew cut hair. The gold name tag over his heart said Winston Smiley, and he was living up to his name. He was smiling from ear to ear when he greeted Jonah and reached out to shake his hand.

"How you doing Jonah? Man, you been gone about two weeks, when we gonna go fishin' again? Howdy Ma'am." He tipped his hat to the young lady sitting next to Jonah.

"Win, I'd like you to meet Dr. Abigail Campbell. She'll be working with us for a while."

"Pleased to meet you Doctor Campbell," Winston saluted her. "Glad to have you aboard."

"Call me Abby."

"Yes Ma'am, I mean Abby," said Win.

"I'll get her set up with a security badge and show her around, and I'll come back out later and we'll talk about fishing."

Winston was beaming, "Alriiightt!"

Jonah pulled through the gate and headed to the parking lot next to the building.

"He sure is a happy sort," said Abby.

"Yeah, he's great to have around, retired Navy Seal. We don't have to worry about the gate when he's on duty, that's for sure, but one thing for sure he's got some stories that would make your hair curl."

"Do you really need an armed guard at the gate?"

"Better safe than sorry. The public version of why we have armed guards and barbed wire fences is to keep out the wackos. We produce over a hundred different strains of bacteria here, with all kinds of applications, from cleaning oil and fuel hydrocarbons, to managing waste water treatment plants, farm and medicinal uses. The city council made this a condition for us to use this facility. They don't want to see any of the product walk away. The real reason is our research and development is some of the best in the world, and we don't want any of our ideas to walk away before we have them patented."

They walked through the double glass doors into an air conditioned environment. The ground floor entrance was tiled with marble and shining, the walls and ceilings gleamed with stainless steel and glass.

"Smells like chlorine," said Abby.

"One of the most important aspects of a bacteria production facility is sanitation. It's funny in a way, we produce spores, and to get the purest strain we have to eliminate all other bacteria. It starts out here at the entrance. This place is wiped down daily in the afternoon when everyone has gone home."

A large reception desk was near the bank of elevators, and an attractive woman was manning the phones. She looked up when Jonah and Abby walked in and waved to them.

"This is Penny, she's the brains of the operation."

Penny blushed, "Oh shush, I just make sure the coffee pot stays full, so to speak. Nice to meet you Abby, I've heard so much about you, and my goodness that submarine. I saw the picture of the cracked glass. Here is your welcome packet." She pulled out a small envelope and handed it to Abby. "You'll find a map of the facility, name tag, security access cards. I'm here at the front from seven in the morning till six at night so if you need anything just give me a call."

"Why thank you," said Abby and she placed the envelope in her carry bag.

"So Jonah, we have all the supplies and equipment you ordered in your lab set up and ready to go. It sounds very intriguing."

"We are going to mix a strange brew Penny," said Jonah.

The phone rang and Penny waved them off to the elevators.

"Our meeting rooms and cafeteria are down here on the ground floor, and the research lab and production facilities are on the top two floors" said Jonah. "It's a pretty small operation, but we're looking at expanding, and we have the room with this building."

Jonah pushed the button and the doors opened immediately with whoosh.

Abby stalled as she looked at the elevator, "Are there stairs?"

"Sure, right on the side there," said Jonah, "but my office and lab are on the third floor."

"I like to stay in shape," she lied.

"Okay, I'm with you," he said and walked over and opened the door to the emergency stairs. "Follow me," he said and began climbing.

He opened the door at the second floor landing and they peeked in. Stainless steel vats for incubating bacteria lined the entire floor behind glass windows. Two workers were monitoring a computer screen, and they waved at Jonah when they saw him.

"Well I guess business is booming," said Jonah, "according to Ross he's signed up half the shipping companies on the west coast to first response contracts, so the boys are getting ahead on product in case we need it."

When they got to the third floor they came out into a long hallway with floor to ceiling glass windows on one side of the hall that looked out onto the city, and the same type of glass wall that looked into the labs.

"There sure is a lot of glass in this building," Abby remarked.

"They used to make aircraft electronics here. It was climate controlled and dust proof, but we came in and upped the ante so to speak, and made it microbe proof. The glass was already here, we just sealed the edges and put in an air system that sort of works like a reverse osmosis filter, it squeezes the air through layers of filters and comes out with only the gas compounds. It even filters out the naturally present water vapour, and so we add a little bit on the inside, otherwise we'd have dry throats all day." He pointed through the glass to some people who were sitting at a lab station with Petri dishes and microscopes. They were wearing total body covering blue suits and full face masks with a hose for an air tank on their back. The people saw them and waved. Jonah gave them the thumbs up.

"They're working on a microbe that will eat industrial solvents that leaked into the groundwater system near a chemical plant in Texas, pretty serious stuff. One whiff of the air from their lungs would contaminate the bug that they're trying to isolate, and so they're wearing those suits. From what I hear they're just about finished with the prototype and they're going to head out to the site next week to test it, so it will just be us at the lab for awhile till they get back."

He stopped at a door. Above it hung a crude sign made from a large flat piece of sun bleached driftwood, and painted on it was a caricature of a big face with red eyes and gaping mouth and teeth that was about to devour an oil rig held tight in its hand.

Under the caricature in ominous dripping black letters were the words 'The Oil Eater'.

"Home sweet home," said Jonah.

"The Oil Eater?" Abby was amused and touched the rough and pitted surface.

"That's me," he beamed. "Can't you see the resemblance?"

She looked closer at the sign and touched one of the letters, it was sticky, and she pulled back her forefinger that was now stained black. "Is that oil?"

He nodded. "Prudhoe Bay Crude. Two hundred and fifty million years old, from the Triassic period. Trapped in a sandstone reservoir nine thousand feet underground, pumped to the surface on the northern coast of Alaska, transported by pipeline to the southern coast, and then spilled by the Exxon Valdez into the clear waters of the gulf. I scraped the oil off the rocks when I was twelve years old and brought it home and made that sign to remind me of what I saw up there. That wood will disintegrate long before the oil will. The only way to get rid of that crude oil is to burn it or feed it to my bugs."

"Charming," she said.

"I made that sign when I was a kid. Pretty good eh? I know what you're thinking. It took a wrong fork in the road when I was young, I should have gone to art school instead of majoring in science right?"

"Yeah that was a mistake alright," as she shook her head. "So you knew what you wanted to be when you were a kid?"

"Sure, doesn't everybody?"

"I wanted to be a ballerina."

"And what happened?"

"I'm a klutz. So, I picked the next best thing, the exciting world of microbiology."

"Well, I'm glad you did," he said with a laugh as he opened the door. "Make yourself at home."

There was a large oak desk in the center of the room, one end piled with files, a large bookcase, pictures along the walls, a huge flat screen TV, refrigerator, putting green, dartboard, punching bag, pool table, wet bar. It was the ultimate man cave.

"A punching bag?"

"Sometimes research gets a little frustrating. And then I take it out on the bag."

"This isn't an office, it's a gym."

"I can tell you like it." He watched as she walked around the room looking at the pictures on the walls. She stopped in front of a black and white picture, a man and a boy stood at the rocky shore of a lake, each one holding up a large trout and smiling.

"Is this you?"

"And my Dad. He liked to fish."

"You had curly hair and dimples."

"I was chubby."

"Well fed."

"And this picture?" She stood in front of another black and white photo of a young woman holding a baby.

"My Mom."

"She's really pretty."

"Twenty five years old. She passed away right after that picture was taken."

"Oh, I'm sorry."

"Don't be."

He opened the refrigerator, took out a small bottled water and offered it to her.

"We also have beer, wine, soda, juice, coffee, tea."

"Water is fine, thank you."

He handed the water to her and grabbed a beer.

"Should we have a game of pool," he asked, "or should we get to work?"

"I'd really like to get started, I mean if that's okay. I'm sure we'll hit some roadblocks on the way and then we can play a round of pool, or punch the bag."

He sat down in the wooden chair at the desk and turned on the computer. "You're right, let's get started. But I have to warn you, once I get going on a project, I don't like to stop until it's completed." He turned the computer screen towards her and motioned to a chair.

She handed him a CD and he loaded it into the computer.

An animated program popped up on the screen, and he opened two images side by side.

"Okay back to work, here's the gene sequence from the bacteria mat next to the deep sea smoker, and here is the sequence from my oil eater."

The two twisting lines were highlighted in color, sections of the DNA strand delineated with blue, red, and green. Jonah pointed to a blue section of Abby's strand.

"This is the section I'm proposing deals with the force pressure, and this," pointing to a green section, " is where I think we'll find the trait ability to survive the oxygen-free environment."

"What about the ability to withstand high heat?"

"I haven't decided."

"Well, I think that beer has clouded your thinking."

Jonah sat back in mock astonishment. "Oh really?"

Abby pointed to sections to the top and bottom of the ones that Jonah had indicated. "Rotate this section."

Jonah used the mouse to maneuver the 3D strand so they were looking at the back side.

"This is the section I believe handles the pressure, and this handles the non oxygen environment."

"And the heat?"

She also shook her head. "Not sure."

"Well we have two educated guesses. Care to make a wager?"

"A what?"

"A wager, a bet, a gamble, a play. The winner receives, and the loser provides a prize, be it cash, an object, or a service."

Abby narrowed her eyes at him. "Alright, you're on mister."

Jonah clapped his hands together, jumped out of the chair and went to the dart board and grabbed the three darts from the red bull's-eye. He stepped back to a line on the floor and tossed the first dart at the board. It just missed the center.

"Okay, so what will it be?" he asked. "A hundred bucks? A fancy dinner with all the trimmings?"

"You're talking to a poor undergraduate student. Let's narrow the parameters," she said. "Loser cleans the lab."

He tossed another dart and it missed the bulls-eye by a hair, the tip bouncing off the metal ring that surrounded the red dot, and clanking to the floor.

"Ouch."

He was down to his last dart, and eyed up the dart board, measuring the distance carefully, and then let the dart fly. He looked over at her as the dart hit the center bull's-eye with a definitive thud.

They both burst into laughter at the absurdity of it all.

"It's just like I always say," said Abby. "People will find a reason to fight over anything they can find, no matter how small."

11.

Abby had three bacteria strains from her trip to the bottom of the sea. One from the mat growing right underneath the black smoker, one from the interior of the tube worms, and one from the gills of a crab she had been able to snag with the robot arm.

Before she'd been fired she isolated the bacteria, and freeze dried them, and while she was travelling and looking for a position in a research lab she stored them all in a little Styrofoam container with dry ice to keep them at thirty six degrees. At that temperature they could last fifteen years and come back as good as new. Every five days she added fresh dry ice to keep the temperature constant, and now that she was finally safe in a real laboratory again they were stored in a normal refrigerator.

"Come to Mommy," she said as she pulled out one of the little containers.

"That's a little weird," he deadpanned.

"You know what I mean."

It was a glass vial the size of her thumb and she set it into a plastic box with holes specially designed to hold it steady and pulled off the plastic lid and carefully injected room temperature purified water with a syringe and replaced the lid.

She repeated the process for the other two types of bacteria, and then brought the first one over to another table where Jonah had laid out two dozen eight inch round Petri dishes with an agar growing solution of animal fats and proteins.

You can fit a thousand bacteria cells on the head of a pin, and combined with the right growing conditions, and enough nutrients the colony will double every ten minutes. At that rate a single bacteria cell would multiply to one hundred thirty one thousand and seventy two cells in just three hours.

With the syringe Abby squirted three straight lines of reactivated bacteria across each Petri dish, a million bacteria per line, moving methodically from dish to dish like a factory worker and careful not to miss a drop. Jonah moved each dish into a specially designed incubator five feet high with glass shelves.

There were ten identical incubators standing next to each other and he took out a sharpie and marked on a little flash card on the top which strain was inside.

They repeated the same procedure with the other two bacteria strains from the bottom of the ocean, and after those were safe and growing in the incubators, they washed up and took a break. The whole procedure had taken a little less than an hour.

She smiled. "What next boss?"

He frowned. "You don't have to call me boss." He hesitated and thought for a moment. "Sir will suffice."

"Well you are a lot older than me."

His frown returned. "And wiser."

"Mostly older."

"Ouch."

She bowed. "Oh, elder wise one, what next?"

"Alright let's recap our game plan. Next thing we do is wait. In three hours those Petri dishes will have billions of live bacteria cells, and then we can start harvesting your strains of bacteria, then we'll separate the DNA from the cells, cut chromosome sections we've identified, and recombine those sections with the Alaska strain."

She looked at the clock, it was almost noon. "Since we have a few hours before we can continue, how about we take a break and play a game of pool?" she suggested. "Loser pays for lunch."

"You're on," he said.

Three hours later, after he'd paid for a pizza delivery they were back in the lab.

Cutting and splicing DNA, unlike what the term implies, does not employ the use of little microscopic knives. The cutting is done with enzymes, chemically acting as the cutting tools, and there are thousands of combinations that will cut the chromosome at a specific point. The key is find the spot in the strand that you want to cut and leave a jagged edge, and then add in the other strand that was taken from a different type of cell and mix them together and bind them with a chemical ligase and form a new strand of DNA. This genetic recombination is then reinserted back into live cells where the new DNA transforms the cell according to the properties that the DNA instructs it.

Day after day they worked in the lab, harvesting and cutting and splicing, recombining and then incubating new strains, then harvesting and testing over and over.

As it turned out, they were both wrong.

A long week later after growing and trimming and cutting and pasting DNA section after section onto the separate bacteria strands, they were nowhere near finding the right combination.

The oil eating bacteria still would not survive any amount of pressure or lack of oxygen, and the frustration was setting in.

Jonah was punching the bag in staccato motion, right left, right left, right left. Sweat was streaming down his face and arms. His mind was at rest, and he let his instincts take over. Right left, right left, right left. His knuckles cracking the leather of the bag as it rebounded at an angle. Right left, right left, right left. He ended it with a big right hook and stood looking blankly at the bag as it slowed to a stop.

"Computer," he shouted. "Turn the air conditioning down to sixty one degrees."

Abby sat at the computer running comparisons. No combo that they have tried has worked. Jonah's oil eating bacteria will not live without oxygen, or at pressure. They can't get it to thrive with pressure and oxygen, no pressure and no oxygen, no pressure with oxygen, not to mention heat. If they give it perfect conditions with oxygen and no pressure and then add heat, it perishes.

"We're going about this the wrong way," said Abby.

"No kidding."

"No, I mean we are really going about this the wrong way."

"And I agree. If we were going about it the right way we'd have at least some success by now."

"What if we turn this around and look at it from the opposite angle?" she asked.

"I'm listening."

"Instead of splicing the deep water microbe's DNA into the oil eating microbe, we go the other route. Take the oil eating trait and place it the deep water microbe"

"I don't think it will work."

"Why not?"

"The oil eating trait is too complex. Your solution is too simple with the traits involved."

"Maybe you're just too hard headed."

"I'm a scientist, I don't get hard headed."

She scoffed.

"Double or nothing?"

"You mean our bet?"

"Yes our bet."

"We're already at nothing owed, since we were both wrong with our original assumptions. You don't know how this gambling thing goes do you?"

"Well then you've got nothing to lose since you're so sure this won't work."

He pulled the darts from the bulls-eye and stepped back and took aim. He tossed the first dart and it went straight in the red center.

"This will take another two weeks to prepare and perform you know."

"I'm okay with that."

He tossed the second dart and it also went directly into the center bulls-eye.

"So if you're wrong, you clean the lab every day. And if you're right I owe you the same?"

"Do we have a deal?"

"I would say this is a slam dunk if it wasn't for the two weeks of prep time. Alright we have a deal." He tossed the third dart and it bounced off the metal surrounding the bulls-eye and clattered on the floor. "Uh oh."

12.

Monroe was able to lease an office space right across the street from the research lab. It was on the second floor above a convenience store, two rooms with heating and air conditioning furnished with desks and chairs and a couch in the first room which had been the waiting room.

The walk through and negotiation with the leasing agent went quickly.

"What type of business was the previous tenant involved in?" he asked the agent.

"Real Estate."

"Oh, and what happened, did they go out of business?"

"No, actually they did quite well, so well in fact that they needed a bigger space, so they moved up to the center of the city."

"Good for them," said Monroe. "I like hearing success stories."

"What business are you in again?"

"Consulting." A real ambiguous answer.

"Oh? What type?" asked the inquisitive agent.

"Stocks, bonds, equities, trusts, real estate, taxes, insurance, the whole ball of wax so to speak. We'll take a company, or individual's entire economic sphere and put it under the microscope and tweak it to maximize their earnings potential. We take the guess work out of the equation."

The listing agent looked impressed. "Maybe I should make an appointment."

"I'm booked solid for two months," said Monroe.

"Dang it. Oh well, what do you think about this space?"

Monroe walked into the second room, tapped on the desk and the walls, and looked out the window at the traffic, and the lab across the street.

"Doesn't seem too noisy."

"No, it's actually very quiet, this is not a busy part of town, and we have double paned windows." He tapped on a window pane for effect.

"What do they do over there?" asked Monroe, pointing to the lab complex.

"You know, I think it's a microbiology lab, something high tech."

"Microbiology? Is there any danger?"

"Oh I doubt it sir; this city is pretty strict with that sort of stuff."

"I see they have a guard shack at the entrance."

"Right, well that's probably just to keep a check on visitors and what not." The agent tried to look at his watch without letting on. These little ticky tack questions weren't going anywhere, he thought, it's an office space pal, take it or leave it. He did have other appointments, and this little lease didn't put much cash into his pocket.

"You mentioned internet access."

"High speed cable." The agent pointed to the outlets near the desk. "It's included in the lease as well as electricity. Phone is not included, although there is an outlet. Most people just use the internet for phone service these days anyways."

Monroe pretended to mull over the place, alternately wincing and nodding and bobbing his head while thinking hard. Couldn't let this person think he was too anxious.

"Alright," he finally pronounced with much fanfare and actually smiled as he said it, "I'll take it!"

The agent let out a little sigh of relief, and smiled broadly. "Great! Let's do the paperwork right now."

Monroe handed him a check from a local bank where he had set up an account in a fictitious name, and he was in business.

He could sleep on the couch and wash up in the bathrooms down the hall that the other businesses on this floor of the building used.

There was a tax accountant, a law office, and a graphic design outfit that all closed their doors at six in the evening so he'd have the place to himself. If he needed a shower he could rent a hotel room for the night. It was just like old times in the CIA.

It took less than an hour to set up the surveillance equipment. First order of business was placing the one way film on the inside of the windows of the second room. This way he could set up a microwave dish to control the bug, and high powered telescopes and audio monitoring devices without anyone on the outside seeing what he was doing.

He installed a privacy bolt on the entry door and also on the door to the second room where he'd be working to keep anyone like the janitor or leasing agent to surprise him.

He waited patiently for over an hour and right on time the FedEx truck arrived with a package that he had set up to be delivered.

He powered up the two flying bugs and synchronized their radio bandwidths with the controller.

They were tiny, about the size of a wasp, with HD cameras and audio and could fly over a mile while being remote controlled. He set the first one on the windowsill and off it went straight for the building across the street. His controller was set up exactly like a computer game console with duel toggles to control the up and down and forward motions. This device after all was designed by the generation that had grown up playing those games. His computer screen showed what the bug saw in real time and flying it was quite easy after some practice.

The high definition cameras on the front of the bug adjusted to the lighting as it entered the front door with the FedEx delivery and flew across the lobby into the open elevator, and he landed on the top corner and attached the bug and waited. The secretary carried the box into the elevator and he flew the bug onto her back and attached it unnoticed. When she carried the box into Jonah's office and bent down to leave it on the desk he flew the bug up onto the ceiling into a dark corner.

He could zoom in on the computer screen on the desk and rotate the cameras to any part of the room for this placement. He turned the power to rest to conserve energy while Jonah and Abby were in the lab area.

An hour later another truck arrived with another delivery and he repeated the process with the second bug. He streamed the visual and audio onto the web server and on the other side of the globe a phone rang.

Moldini answered.

"We're in," was all Moldini heard and Monroe hung up and went back to monitoring the feed. He watched Jonah and Abby at work through the telescope and waited. Soon there would be an opening and he would fly the second bug into the lab and leave the first one in the outer office.

13.

Another long week later Jonah and Abby sat huddled around the computer screen in the outer office.

They looked at the data together, the numbers scrolling across the computer screen; it was kind of like unwrapping a present on Christmas morning and their hopes were high, only this time the box was empty. The bacteria had not survived.

Jonah took off his reading glasses and rubbed his aching eyes. "Another failed attempt."

Abby printed the results and closed the computer program, and looked at the clock. It was exactly ten in the morning on the seventh day of their efforts. "It's still early; we can try another sequence before lunch."

Jonah paced the length of the lab and looked out the window. "This is getting us nowhere. We're guessing on sequences. We need a break." He looked at her, "I need a break."

She took that to mean he needed a break from being around her. "Oh," she said. "I can take a walk and get some lunch or something, and give you your space."

He laughed. "I don't need a break from you! I need a break from this." He waved his hand at the lab. "My mind gets dull if I think too much, and boy am I dull now. I need to go outside and look around at the world, and not think, if that makes sense."

She didn't know what to say and shifted on her toes.

"I have a boat nearby," he said, "for situations just like this. Have you ever been fishing on a boat?"

"Not unless you count fishing for bacteria at the bottom of the ocean."

"Ah, well Abigail Campbell you are in for a treat." He grabbed the phone and dialed the gate house while looking out the window. Win answered the phone, and Jonah could see him answering the phone through the gate house window. "What do you say we take the yacht out for a spin Win? See if we can hook a few before lunch."

Win gave a fist punch and looked out the gatehouse door and up towards the lab, a big smile on his face. "Now we're talking!" he practically yelled into the phone.

They loaded Jonah's jeep with bags of ice and sodas and sandwiches and headed for the nearby dock.

Through the industrial center across a bridge and at the south end of a nearby island was a small marina with over a hundred boats and yachts tied to the docks. There were five short docks with slips for ten boats on either side, and two long docks with slips for twenty five boats on a single side. Jonah's twenty five foot Bayliner was parked halfway down one of the smaller docks, and he pulled the jeep on the road near the entrance.

Win was beaming as he carried the ice in one arm and the sodas in another.

"You really like going fishing don't you?" Abby asked him as they walked down the wooden planks that made up the dock.

"Oh yes ma'am. I go fishing every day that I can rain or shine, and here in Seattle as you know it's more rain than shine. But I don't mind one bit if it's rainy or not, I just love being outside by the water. I make my own lures, and fish on the shoreline most of the time, unless someone invites me out on their boat. I've been saving up for my own boat, little by little, and I should have enough by the end of the year. Jonah says I can take his boat out any time I want to, but every time in my life that I've borrowed something I usually break it, so I won't take the chance, no way."

Win was a strapping good looking young man with short brownish hair and big ears. His cheeks had a perpetual ruddy rose color and his eyes were as blue and untroubled as a clear sky.

"How old are you Win?" asked Abby.

"Twenty two, ma'am."

"Well I'm only twenty seven, so there's no need to call me ma'am; it makes me feel like I'm a hundred years old. You can call me Abby, that's what all my friends call me."

"Yes, sorry ma'am, I mean... Abby." He blushed as he corrected himself, his normally ruddy complexion blazing in redness.

"Win was in the Marines," said Jonah. "Special forces, Iraq, Afghanistan."

"Leavenworth," continued Win, and his face turned serious, the ruddy color fading. "That's a military prison," he explained to Abby. "Otherwise known as the Unites States disciplinary barracks in Fort Leavenworth, Kansas."

Abby was almost afraid to ask. "What did you do?"

He stopped walking and looked her straight in the eyes. "It's not so much what I did; it's what I didn't do."

He paused and looked at the sky for a moment, he seemed caught in an emotional quandary, and then he took a deep breath and continued.

"My best friend in the platoon was killed by sniper fire one fine afternoon in the Helmond province, southern Afghanistan one month into my tour. We had just delivered an aid package to a little village in the mountains, two hundred pounds of food, clothes, chocolates, books, medicine; you know the usual good stuff. It was a dusty little village in the middle of nowhere, it was dry and cold and dirty, but the people seemed happy, they were smiling and thankful for the gifts, I finally felt like I was doing something good. As we were walking back to our armored convoy my buddy's head was blown off, some bastard high up on the mountain shot him, and I carried him on my shoulders running to our trucks. The captain called in an airstrike and ordered us to counter attack the mountain, but I couldn't move."

"The next day we were mobilizing to hit a target in the same general area and I still couldn't move. It's like I was frozen. I'd been in combat, seen a lot of bad things happen, being part of making bad things happen, but for some reason this was different, we'd just delivered presents for God's sake, like we were Santa Claus or something, and they still shot him. I couldn't go on anymore, I was done. They sent me to psychiatric evaluation, and when I was in the hospital clinic my platoon sergeant came in yelling at me calling me a traitor and a coward and ordered me outside. I broke his jaw with a single punch. I was court marshalled, dishonourably discharged and sentenced to spend two years in prison. They had to make an example of me."

"That's terrible," said Abby.

Win smiled. "It was pretty good actually, kind of like I was in purgatory for my sins, and when I finally came out, into the sun again, I came out clean. And that's why I like to go fishing. I can never forget the past and what's happened, but fishing helps me forget a little bit."

Abby could see now that his blue eyes, though untroubled and clear, were much older than his twenty two years of age.

"Jonah found me living in a little tent next to the dock and fishing and offered to take me out trolling one day, and the next thing I know he offered me a job."

Abby looked with admiration at Jonah who had walked ahead, "Oh he did, did he?"

They were standing in front of a shiny boat with blue trim and a small fly bridge at the end of the dock.

"Well, here she is," said Jonah, pride evident in his voice. On the side of the boat in black letters were the words, 'King Fisher'.

"The King Fisher?"

He helped Abby get aboard and then climbed onboard with the fishing poles and set them into the holders on the stern and attached the safety lines to the eyes on the reels. Win loaded the ice and sodas into the coolers on board and then cast off the bow and stern lines as the engines came to life.

There was a fighting chair in the back and Jonah offered Abby the seat. Jonah manoeuvred the boat away from the dock and out into the channel, and when he was good distance from the dock he revved the engines and soon they were blazing, under the bridge and out into open water of Puget Sound. Winston was standing up on the fly bridge, his hair flying in the breeze scanning the horizon for packs of seabirds which would mean schools of feeding fish.

The sky was clear and the aroma of salt water from the spray off the stern filled the boat. Winston yelled loudly and pointed far out into the bay where the other boats had gathered, and Jonah cranked the wheel and headed out to sea.

When they had gotten within a half mile of the boats they could see hundreds of little black birds flying in flocks by the surface, larger white seagulls ranging and wheeling about, and high above soared the frigate birds, the birds of prey with sharp angled wings built for speed that would swoop down from the heights and steal the fish from the other birds when it suited them.

Winston jumped down from the flying bridge and attached a lure to each of the three poles and one by one let them out the line and set the drag. They were trolling now at a slow pace and circling outside of the other boats, some of which were stationary as the occupants fought fish on their lines and the others also trolling in big circles around the bird pile.

The pole on the right side bent and the line screamed out. Abby nearly jumped out her seat at the sudden sound of it. Jonah kept the boat at a steady speed straight ahead to set the hook and Winston quickly reeled in the other empty lines to keep them out of the fighting area.

"Are you ready?" he shouted to Abby.

"What, me?" she shouted back.

"Yes, you!" he said excitedly as he unlatched the safety hook and handed the fishing pole to her.

Jonah stopped the boat's engines, and the line went straight out from the fighting chair and then started going sideways as the fish ran.

Winston was elated. "That's it! You got him."

She cranked the reel and then held on tight as the fish made one last run, the line screaming from the reel and then stopped like a dead weight was on the other end.

Winston was encouraging "Now's your chance, reel 'em in!"

She cranked and cranked and cranked the reel, and soon they could see the silver flash near the surface as the fish came up. Winston grabbed the hand net with one hand and the line with other and with one swift motion dipped the net into the sea and out came a thrashing salmon. Winston brought it on board and with the nearby bat gave it one quick bap on the top of its head and it flopped once and lay still on the deck.

"Nice one!" he exulted and extended his hand for a high five.

"I caught it!" said Abby.

Jonah smiled as he watched her, and then he put the boat in gear again. Winston tossed the salmon into the cooler and piled the ice on top of it, and then let out the three lines again as he let out a whoop. "Fishing from a boat is waaay better than on land!"

They landed four more salmon, and then the birds suddenly disappeared along with the fish. They trolled slowly back towards the wharf. Jonah asked Winston to take the wheel and he gladly obliged. Jonah sat towards the back near Abby who still sat in the fighting chair.

"Now I know why you like fishing so much," she said.

"Pretty exciting huh? Well, it's not always this good, and that's why they call it fishing and not catching. But we did catch five nice ones today, enough for us and enough to share."

"Feel better now?' she asked.

He just nodded and watched the lines as they cut through the water behind the boat. Beads of liquid climbed the lines as they went taught and straight and humming through the sea. She could see that he was at peace now but somehow by the looks of him his mind was racing.

He pointed to the lines cutting through the water, and looked over at her. "I've got it."

"What do you mean you've got it?"

"I mean I think I've got it. It just came to me, watching the lines, the way they cut through the water, and the tension of the water causing it to climb backwards up the line."

"That's physics," she said. "It's simple."

"It is simple," he said, "and that's what makes it so amazing. We've been going in the wrong direction. We need to simplify the DNA splice."

He quickly reeled in the lines and unclipped the lures. "Winston," he shouted, "full speed ahead back to port!" He sat at the gunwale next to Abby as the boat reared back with the bow high out of the water and sprinted back to the marina with the engines roaring. "We have to get back to the lab," he said to her and winked.

Later that day they isolated and spliced the DNA following the diagram hastily drawn on the chalk board by Jonah. It was a simple mix. They watched as the bacteria began to multiply on the Petri dishes arranged in the incubator.

Placed over one of the Petri dishes was a microscope which was routed by cable to a computer screen nearby. Jonah nudged the controls to bring the image into crisp focus and turned on the camera that would take an image every second for the next ten hours and give them a time lapse movie of the bacteria as it multiplied.

"Looks like they're doubling every ten minutes, right on schedule," said Jonah. "They'll be in the millions within a few hours, and billions by the morning."

He looked over Abby and her eyes were droopy.

"I'm exhausted," she said.

"Fishing will do that to you." He snapped his fingers. "I almost forgot about the salmon!"

He looked out the window and could see the cooler still sitting in the back of the pickup truck. Win was long gone and the gate was locked. When they'd gotten back from fishing Win had transferred his split of the catch into his cooler and detailed to them how he was going to cook it with wine and olive oil and spices and lemon on the side. Jonah had barely listened to him and was focused on getting up to the drawing board lab and splicing some DNA.

Now that the deed was done and the new strain of bacteria happily growing his thoughts went back to Win's recipe, and the fresh salmon in the cooler.

"I don't know about you but I'm starving."

"I could eat," she said.

They left the light on inside the incubator and it cast a glow onto the drawing on the chalkboard.

There was a buzzing in the air as the flying bug attached itself to the ceiling and observed the scene below with the chalkboard and computer screen and the bacteria crawling across it.

Jonah and Abby left through the gate and locked it behind them and went to Jonah's apartment for salmon steaks and potatoes and an early night.

14.

Early the next morning they arrived back at the lab. Winston was in fine form at the gate and gave them a crisp military salute as they drove through.

"Thanks for taking me fishing yesterday Jonah."

"We've got some work to do this morning, but maybe later today we can drag some lines."

They opened the door to the lab and turned on the lights. All was quiet as they looked at the incubator. The Petri dishes were covered with the white slime of bacteria.

"Holy cow," said Jonah, "they've been busy."

He clapped his hands together and sat at the computer and dragged an icon with the photos from the microscope into a movie editing program; one photo per second over the course of ten hours equaled thirty six thousand photos. He checked a box on the first photo indicating 'open as image sequence' and now they had a time lapse movie of the bacteria multiplying. He squeezed the footage down so that the ten hours played back in ten seconds.

"Check this out," he said to Abby who was still looking at the Petri dishes.

The bacteria, little single celled round creatures danced and caroused and piled high on top of each other in the thousands in rapid fire action and came so close to the microscope that it went out of focus towards the end of the sequence.

"They sure are a lively bunch, we got that part right." said Abby. "Now let's see how they can do under pressure."

"This is the fun part," said Jonah as he scanned the lab. "Alright what's it going to be today?" Under an adjacent table were five gallon buckets filled with crude oil and tar and alluvial sand and rock, all mixed together like slush, pretty much what you would find in a typical reservoir of oil far beneath the surface of the earth, or in a marsh or back eddy of a waterway that had been hit with an oil spill.

He pointed to a container near the end of the line and read the label out loud. "Prudhoe Bay Crude".

"One of my favorites," she agreed.

He scooted it out and popped the top off. Some of the black goo was stuck to the bottom of the lid and he was careful not to touch it.

Lined along the table above the buckets were ten bright gallon sized stainless steel canisters with boltable lids that had pressure hoses attached to the tops which snaked off the table to the compressor. Each metal lid also had a pressure gauge which was controlled by a computer.

Jonah put one end of a hose into the bucket and the other into the first canister. In the middle of the hose was a hand crank and as he turned it the oil slush filled the metal canister to the half gallon line on the inside. Ten canisters later and they were ready for the bacteria. Abby had scraped the bacteria from the Petri dishes and into a large container. From the ten bacteria they had created, they now had millions that filled a cup sized beaker.

"Would you like the honor?" asked Abby.

"Be my guest," said Jonah and waved as he bowed towards the canisters.

The bacteria were suspended in a clear liquid and Abby carefully measured out each dose with a syringe, fifteen millilitres around one table spoon each which she emptied into the center of each canister on top of the oil slush.

When she was finished she put the remaining bacteria in another stainless steel container and put that into the freeze dry machine so they could preserve the strain without it multiplying out of control. Jonah was busy bolting the lids down tight with a specially fitted wrench. The canisters could withstand thousands of pounds of pressure, and the plan was to stagger the pressure from sea level to an extreme of three thousand feet.

Abby stood by as the last canister lid was secured.

"Ready?" Jonah asked.

"Fire it up," she said.

Jonah flipped the switch on the compressor and it hummed as it gathered air and pumped it into the lines. The needles in the pressure gauges began rise with the first canister registering zero, the next one twenty pounds, and then forty, then eighty doubling in pressure until the tenth canister registered five thousand one hundred and ten pounds per square inch.

Abby winced "I sure hope that last canister holds."

"Yeah, me too," Jonah admitted. "Let's at least start the process of freeze drying that strain and go get a bite to eat."

Freeze drying bacteria is a common method to preserve a strain. First you need to freeze the culture and then slowly dry it out in a vacuum. It was a two step process that sometimes necessitated multiple pieces of equipment. Lucky for them they had a single machine that could do it all. Abby put the vial into the chamber and turned the machine on, the freezing mist from the dry ice entered the chamber and the temperature inside was instantly minus one hundred and nine degrees Fahrenheit, freezing solid the little bacteria. The machine then switched off the dry ice, pumped all the air out to create a vacuum chamber and slowly heated to dry the material out. For such a small amount it would take less than five hours, just about the amount of time they needed to measure the live bacteria inside the pressurized canisters and determine whether they would thrive, or die in the minimal to the harshest conditions that they were subjected to.

Abby and Jonah went down to the little cafeteria for a bite to eat and when they came back...

They slowly let the pressure out of the canisters and prepared to measure the results. Each canister measured the carbon dioxide content of the air to see how much the bacteria had expelled.

"Un...believable."

The chart on the computer showed them what they already knew when they emptied the canisters and could see with their own eyes that the amount of bacteria to oil increased as they went down the line. The last canister held only sand and rock and no bacteria remained. The test confirmed it. In five hours the canister with the highest pressure had eaten all the oil and completely died off from lack of nutrients.

They measured the oil content in each of the canisters and plugged the data into the program.

The bacteria's efficiency increased the more pressure that was applied.

They did a double test to check the data, and the results were the same.

15.

Moldini was sitting in his air conditioned office watching the computer screen when the phone rang. It was Monroe.

"Did you get the latest feed?"

"Of course," said Moldini, "I've been watching it all morning,"

"It looks like they succeeded in their experiment."

"It appears so."

"What do you want me to do?"

"Stay put, keep monitoring the situation."

"The batteries in the flies are running down. I've been shutting them down at night when no one is at the lab, but they're wearing down quick. It's night time now and they're shut down."

"How much time is left?"

"A day at the most and then I'll need to fly them out for a recharge."

"Fly them out?" Idiot, thought Moldini. "Keep them where they're at," he said. "I think we've seen enough, but I want to know what their next move will be, now that they've created their little monster. Keep the flies in place and only power them up when Jonah is in the lab."

There was silence on the other end of the line.

"Do you understand?" said Moldini. A vein was throbbing on his forehead as he spoke.

"Understood."

Moldini hung up the phone and stroked his goatee as he looked out the window at the oil fields spread out across the desert as the sun rose in the East.

"What now Jonah?" he wondered out loud. "What now?"

16.

Tariq Azul was a small bear of a man with a thick grey beard, and stout midsection, and was the chief of security for the oil conglomerate. Born in Morocco and raised in Beirut, he was the youngest son of a well known medical Doctor. He was small in size and was bullied throughout his young life, by his five older brothers and everyone else it seemed.

Eventually it created a fighting spirit in him as though it was him against the entire world. A turning point in his life came one night at the dinner table when he was thirteen. His brothers were haranguing him again, and he could take it no more, and so he lunged across the table and grabbed the nearest antagonist by the throat, choking him on the ground and kicking off the others as they tried to wrest him from his prey.

Finally his father used a pressure point hold on his wrist to pry him free. The dishes were all scattered, his mother was crying, every older brother had a black eye or split lip from his kicks, and he was sent to his room without food, but the older brothers never picked on him again.

He went to a liberal University in Britain as a language major where he was quickly radicalized, and then rebelling against his father's wishes he fought in Afghanistan, Iraq, and Syria.

Fluent in Russian and English as well as his native tongues of Arabic, Hebrew, Persian and other Middle East languages, he was recruited by and worked for both the CIA and the KGB during the cold war. He played both sides against each other and became a major force in intelligence gathering as he gathered various conspirators around him. It was a dirty business, and he created a circle of killers, thieves and spies across the whole Middle East.

Like a crime organization, they extorted money from the foreign governments for protection and information. After a time he was approached by the oil magnates, for his reputation had grown, and they needed help from time to time. The money they offered was much, much more than he could make by squeezing the foreigners and so he disbanded his organization and brought the best of his team with him.

Oil was the biggest business in this part of the world, and there were many perils to confront. The money involved was immense and therefore the potential for graft and extortion was also immense, there were thieves large and small circling the oil profits like wolves and hyenas circle the deer. Now however, a different kind of peril had emerged. He looked across the table and spoke slowly and methodically.

"It has come to our attention that a threat has arisen."

Moldini sat in the opposite chair and responded carefully.

"Perhaps, you have seen the tape?"

Of course he had seen the surveillance tape. The moment Moldini asked this question he knew it was foolish to think otherwise.

"Some, but not all. Why didn't you contact us?"

Moldini bit his lip.

"I was still analysing the data." Another foolish answer.

"What data?" asked Tariq. "It came straight from this Jonah's mouth that this microbe can eat all the oil in the world. It's on the tape."

"I know. It seems impossible. It appears from their testing that the microbe survives and thrives at deep depths under tremendous pressure and with no light or oxygen. Their initial testing was to create a microbe that could eat oil from the surface to a few meters below the soil, but they succeeded in pushing the envelope so to speak."

Tariq looked at Moldini with ice in his eyes.

"So if what you are saying is true, they have created a bacterium that can spread throughout an underground reservoir and devour all the oil it comes in contact with?"

"Well, theoretically yes, but…"

"Isn't a theory merely an idea that needs implementation to become a fact?"

"I don't think it's plausible, yes there is the outside chance that they have created something that could possibly, maybe do what you have suggested..."

"I'm not in the business of taking chances Dr. Moldini, outside chance or not. If there is any possibility of something getting in our way, disrupting our flow of money and with that money our power, I eliminate that potential. Just imagine one of our rivals, the Iranians, or the Russians getting their hands on this thing. They could wipe out our reserves, put us out of business, and then they would control our world. I cannot, we, cannot allow that to happen."

Tariq itched at the chin under his beard as he stared out the window.

"No one else must know of this," he said

"Of course not," replied Moldini. He might yet get out of this alive he thought. But what of Jonah?

"We'll have to send the Fox."

"Yes," agreed Moldini as sweat beaded on his forehead. The Fox meant one thing, assassination. Moldini did not agree with this development, but now he had his own preservation to consider. In fact he was in danger himself. The methodology of creating this microbe was within his ability, and although he lacked the ingredients he had seen the recipe. An impossible recipe and yet it was now a recipe for disaster for Jonah and Abby.

As if on cue and as though Tariq was reading his mind.

"Can you replicate this microbe?" he asked Moldini.

Should he lie, or tell the truth? Of course he could replicate it, but Tariq did not know that, or did he? It would take time and resources, but it could be done, eventually. With Tariq it was best to tell the truth, the alternative was torture.

"Yes," he finally answered.

"Good," said Tariq. "First we'll try to obtain the microbe intact, and if that is not possible, then you will duplicate it.

"But why would you want such a thing?"

Tariq's face lacked emotion as he spoke. "We have enemies around the globe my good Doctor, competitors in our business, who share in the profits, but do not share our views."

So that was it, thought Moldini. They would use the microbe to destroy their competitors' oil reserves, and reap the reward, since the less oil available, the higher the price. What started out as a simple plan to steal a fellow scientist's creation had become a plot to control and dominate the world.

"I'm ready at any time," said Moldini.

"Good, now if you'll excuse me I have some other business to attend."

Moldini left the room and another man entered and closed the door behind him.

"Where is the Fox?" asked Tariq.

"Saint Tropez," replied the man.

"Enjoying himself no doubt."

"Most likely."

"Get word to him at once. I have a very important job for him."

17.

Philip Weintraub, AKA the Fox sat under an umbrella on the veranda of a café on the outskirts of the seaside town of Saint Tropez. A young man in his late twenties, his sand colored hair clean cut, and with a vibrant smile, he looked like an American college kid fresh out of school.

He had a scar that ran from his left cheek bone to his chin, the result of a disagreement when he was in the military. He nodded at all the ladies that passed by with a "Howdy Ma'am," in a Texan drawl to the older women, and a "Good morning Miss," with a wink to the younger ones. He wore a crisp Aloha shirt, khaki shorts, leather sandals and aviator sunglasses, and no one would suspect that he was an international killer.

The waiter came to his table and inquired in French if he would like another drink.

"Oui, oui my good man," in his best fake French accent, and handed him the empty bottle of beer.

The waiter nodded and walked away and as he walked back to the bar he shook his head and thought what an ass that tourist is, heralding all the women who walked by and looking like a buffoon. But he had tipped well the past couple of days so he would tolerate him with a smile as well as he could.

Philip watched the waiter walk away and knew what he was thinking. The French were famous at snobbery, the men at any rate to other men from different countries. They excelled at it; in fact it was almost like a national pastime, like baseball in America, or soccer in Brazil. It didn't bother Philip one bit, it intrigued him. Little did that little waiter know that he could snap his spine with a single tap of his knuckles.

Philip loved Saint Tropez, he loved everything about it, the seaside location, the restaurants, bars, hotels, but most of all the people, he was above all else a people watcher, almost like a student of people and this was a big giant classroom. They walked by the café all day long going here and there, sometimes stopping and sitting for drinks or food. From his perch at the end of the veranda he could see the sweeping beach to the south, the road running along the sea, and the giant yachts parked in the calm blue bay out front. The rich and the not so rich could mingle and roam the avenues in search of diversion.

He had heard of Russian oligarchs spraying fifteen thousand dollar magnums of champagne into the crowds, movie stars frolicking in the clubs. He was more interested in the commoners, the ones barely getting by and he imagined what their lives were like as they passed.

Born of Jewish Americans in New York, his parents immigrated to Israel when he was a baby.

Graduating from high school in Tel Aviv with honours and serving in the military for two years as required, he found himself at twenty one years of age highly trained, bursting with energy, and bored. He joined some fight clubs and found that he enjoyed hand to hand combat.

He fought in a two short wars against the Arabs, but then there was a time of semi peace, with no action, stuck in a garrison with a penny pinching supply clerk monitoring and rationing how many rounds of ammo he could fire in practice. And so he quit the Israeli military and went out on his own and became a mercenary. He acquired an American passport as was his birthright, and unchallenged as he would be with an Israeli model, he could travel at will.

Pinned down by mortar fire one sunny day in Bahrain, he found himself sharing a cubby hole in a blown out building with the son of an Arab sheik. The rag tag militia that he worked for was under fire from the government forces. The young boy was out chasing rabbits with a pellet gun, got caught in the cross fire and holed up in the nearest building he could find. He showed Philip his ID.

"My father is the richest man in the country," he boasted as well as he could while shaking with fear.

"Don't worry," said Philip. "I'm not in the business of harming the young."

A short while later a small gang of the rebel forces he was working for stormed into the building also seeking shelter from the mortars and seeing the young boy realized they had a trophy of war in their grasp. They aimed their weapons at the young man and Philip made a split second decision, and dispatched them all in a hail of bullets. Firing at close range was his specialty, and he was the best.

The next thing he knew he had a job with the sheik, providing protection for the family. One thing led to another and his job of providing protection grew from that little cubby hole to the world.

The air in Saint Tropez in the afternoon smelled of the sea and tanning lotion, sweet and salty at the same time, the old and the new, the ancient brew of the ocean briny and acrid and hard from which all life emerged and the sultry oil from a lotion smoothed on young skin lounging on the sands and besides the pools dotting the coast. Add to that canvas of scent the subtle wafting of smoke and barbecue, garlic roasting in pans of butter, and champagne and wine. If you closed your eyes and your ears you could almost imagine that you were in the midst of any seaside city of the ancient Greek or Roman empires.

There had been a small crime wave since he'd been in town. In fact just about every town he visited experienced a crime wave while he was there. It wasn't a coincidence; he just got a little bored wherever he went, and would go out and rob a store, or blow up a bank, or steal a car to get the old adrenaline going. It was fun.

Philip was admiring two tall brunettes walking by and giggling. They wore summer dresses and were speaking in one of the Slavic languages, deep and rounded sounds that got his blood boiling.

"Mademoiselles," he called out to them in his finest French accent. They smiled at him but kept walking and laughed with each other at some whisper that they exchanged.

Oh well, he thought, there's always more fish in the sea, or girls on the beach, or beer in the glass. He took another sip of the beer in front of him and waited. The sun was getting lower on the horizon, the colors becoming golden and soft. This was his favorite time of the day, probably because night time was just around the corner, and night time meant the excitement of the chase, or the odd explosion or two.

Another pretty girl was walking down the sidewalk towards the café, and this one was casually glancing around as she walked, swerving her curves, tossing her hair and throwing furtive glances to the sides as though she were looking around to see if anyone was looking at her. She was dressed in a polka dot dress with a large flowing white hat and her long brown hair covered her tanned shoulders and down to the middle of her back.

"Hello love," he said to her as she passed, and she stopped and smiled at him. Sometimes the casual direct approach worked best.

"Hello," she said with a light French accent, and came closer, curious, "do we know each other?"

"Absolutely not," he replied. "It's the first time in my life I've ever seen such a beautiful girl as you."

Her smile brightened, and he knew he had her. She was his for the taking.

Then he gave her the same old line that he always gave a girl if she would give him the time, and most often it worked like a charm. It was like the old saying, that girls just wanted to have fun.

"I'm new here in town," he continued. "Would you like to have dinner and perhaps show me around, maybe see a movie or a play?"

She bit her lower lip as though thinking it over, and he put on his best hopeful honest look, eyes wide like a puppy dog.

"How about if we have a drink together," he said, "and talk about it. It's a nice evening and it would be a shame to spend it alone."

He got up and pulled back a chair for her.

"Well, that sounds nice," she said and sat at the table opposite of him.

He always decided in advance over a cup of coffee and a newspaper in the morning what fake name he would be using, and Antoine was it for today. Antoine had just been elected Mayor of a little village outside of Paris, read a small article in the paper, and half the town was up in arms. Antoine was a rascal.

"My name is Antoine," he said and held his hand out.

"Anna," she replied, and briefly held his hand in greeting.

The waiter looked over at the scene that was unfolding as he cleaned a nearby table and frowned. 'How does this arrogant ass do it?' he thought. Every day he comes into the café and he ends up leaving with a different girl who is more beautiful than the one before her. Maybe he has some French blood in him after all he surmised, after all, that could be the only answer to explain it. He walked over and bowed to the lady.

"And something for you Mademoiselle?"

"Champagne."

"And you Monsieur, another beer?"

"Oui," said Philip. He sat back and admired her beauty. "Do you live in this town?"

She was soft spoken. "Why yes, I was here to meet with a friend, but she got called away on business at the last minute."

"Such a shame for her to miss such a nice sunset."

"And you Antoine? That is a French name, but you are not French?"

It was more of a statement than a question, and he hesitated for a moment before answering.

"No, I'm an American. I'm also here on business, and as fate would have it, was in the right place at the right time, wouldn't you agree." He winked at her and she smiled.

"Why yes," she said and blushed. "So you are here on business, how exciting to travel for work. What type of business are you in?"

Unnecessary questions, but not to be unexpected. Why couldn't the women just sit there and look pretty? He hid his disdain for her prying into his life, and kept his smile intact. "I'm in the shipping business, packing and shipping. Yes, I'm here to negotiate a contract with a local company, I don't want to get into the details. Very hush, hush, top secret and all."

She giggled at that and put her finger to her lips. "Oops."

"And what about you mademoiselle Anna, what is the most amazing thing about you that you can tell me."

The waiter was placing the glass of champagne in front of Anna when Philip's phone beeped once.

Someone had sent him a text. Maybe it was the blond Norwegian girl he had met at the club last night. He pulled the phone out of his pocket as a new cold beer was placed on the table in front of him, the moisture sweating on the glass. He nodded and paused until the waiter walked away.

"Cheers," he said and clinked glasses with Anna. She really was quite stunning, but that blond from the club was out of this world. "Please pardon me while I check this message," he said. "I'm expecting a business call."

He flipped the phone open and pushed the button to reveal the text. It was a jumble of letters, numbers and symbols. So, it wasn't the blond from the club. It was an algorithmic code, impossible for anyone to read without the key. But for him it was easy. The keyboard on his phone was in fact the key, along with the predetermined sequence. He went through the code little by little, over five down one, back three up two, and on and on until he had the word.

Seattle.

He had a job.

The details would be stored in an encrypted message on a website that he would gain access to when he got to his laptop at the hotel. It had been quite awhile since his last assignment, five months to the day in fact. Not long enough to get completely rusty, but long enough to lose a little edge. His daily crime spree kept him a little bit up to speed, but there was nothing like assassination for hire to really get you going. It usually involved a near death experience for him as well, which only added to the spice. Whenever they called he had one day to get to the target, and his adrenaline started to flow anticipating the chase.

"Sorry love," he said to Anna as he stood and gave her a wink. "Some other time maybe."

She frowned in disappointment as he dropped some bills on the table and walked away without touching the beer.

There was a shooting range nearby and he headed there to unload a few clips before booking his flight to America.

Yes, he had a job, and it put a bounce in his step.

18.

"Let's look at the facts," said Jonah, "this strain gains potency the more pressure is applied to it, and so in theory could eat oil at the subsurface, and continue down through the strata to perhaps thousands of feet below the surface, and the rate at which it multiplies is astounding. It's increasing its' multiplication with increased pressure, it's actually thriving on it."

"Now we can to test it with other types of hydrocarbons, the kind that might be found on other planets," said Abby.

He stifled a laugh.

"What," she was a little miffed, "you don't think that's a viable experiment?"

"Well, I think it's a little..." he motioned with his forefingers in the air, "out there."

"Hey, you knew going into this partnership what my intentions were for the hyper strain."

"I know, I know, I'm sorry, I didn't mean to imply... It's just that I've been searching for this strain for most of my life and now that I have it," he corrected himself, "now that we have it, I want to test it in a real life situation, like tomorrow. Do you realize what this means? All that oil and tar that's been sitting in places where there's been oil spills like Prudhoe Bay, and the Everglades, pristine beautiful country and it just sits there under the surface like a time bomb waiting for a wave or a flood to bring it to the surface again."

"I know, I'm sorry Jonah, you've been working hard on this for a long time, and I'm just a newbie that got lucky."

"We got lucky."

"Well, our choices are pretty clear. Either we can both go out in the field, or I can go out alone and test it while you stay here and experiment with the compounds you want to ."

Her eyes narrowed as she considered it. "You mean I can stay here and experiment with a long shot, while you take our creation into the field and potentially confirm a ground breaking discovery?" She shook her head. "Not a chance."

"Well, I'm not staying here; I need to get out there…"

"Out there?

"You know what I mean, out in the field."

"Fine, we'll go together."

"Girls are funny."

"Why?"

"You're never quite satisfied."

They worked throughout the day making batches of cultures and filling all the incubators in the lab. In all there were now three hundred Petri dishes swarming with the strain they nicknamed OE57, which stood for 'Oil Eater number fifty seven', the fifty seventh strain they had created over the past two weeks.

19.

The next day they scraped and freeze dried the entire arsenal of bacteria and filled five quarter gallon stainless steel and hermitically sealed canisters to transport to the Gulf of Alaska.

Jonah's plan was simple; they would travel the next day by bush plane to an area that he had worked on in the past. It was trashed with leftover oil from the Prudhoe Bay spill twenty five years earlier where the oil had seeped into the sandy soil near a river mouth. Like much of the coast it was impossible to completely clean.

During times of high rain, or storms with high waves, great swathes of soil were removed and the oil was washed out and into the water again, and it was just like having another spill all over again. They would take core samples of the sandy soil to confirm the presence of the oil residue, and then in close proximity they would activate and sprinkle the OE 57 on the surface in some areas and inject it into others to a depth of five feet. They would then let it work for three days before taking more core samples, and if all went well they would be documenting a breakthrough in science and conservation.

They powered down the lab, cleaned all the surfaces and locked the computer system and when it was all done Jonah packed the OE57 canisters into a large backpack.

"Alright," he said. "I've got the plane all packed up, gassed up, and ready to go, the only thing left to bring is these canisters of OE57."

"Did you pack any chocolate?"

"Nope, no chocolate."

"I have to have some chocolate."

"Why?"

"To celebrate."

"There's nothing to celebrate yet."

"Well then as a pre-celebration."

"There's nothing to pre-celebrate. We're scientists Abby, we don't pre-celebrate. We collect data and analyze it, and if we get the results we want, then we celebrate... with beer."

"Alright, alright I just want some chocolate, because I like it. It makes me happy."

"It's the nitric oxide in the cocoa bean that increases your blood flow that makes you happy."

"You take all the fun out of it."

"Hey I'm a scientist, it's what we do."

"So, do you have any old chocolate bars lying around here, in a drawer or refrigerator or freeze dried in a back room somewhere?"

He shook his head and sighed. "I don't like chocolate."

"Now you tell me." She looked out the window and across the street at the convenience store on the corner. "I'll bet they have chocolate. I'll be right back."

He watched her walk out of the lab, like she was in a hurry to catch a bus or something. "Girls are funny," he said.

It was mid day and she walked sort of fast paced towards the gate. Winston had his chair propped against a wall in the guard house and was reading a fishing magazine and wasn't paying much attention to anything else as Abby quickly walked past him waving and saying hello. He nearly fell off his chair, and caught himself red-faced and stood at attention throwing the magazine to the side. "Hi Abby..."

She stopped just past the gate. "I'm going to that little store to get some chocolate bars, do you want one?"

"Um, sure, here I'll give you some money." He started reaching into his back pocket.

"Never mind," she said as she checked the traffic and continued trotting across the street. "What kind do you like?" she shouted.

"Uh, any kind." He was caught off guard.

"Dark, or light?" She was nearly across the street.

"Dark," he shouted. "With almonds." He smiled. What a gal he thought. Smart, pretty, and she was going to buy him a chocolate bar, with almonds. Too bad she likes Jonah, he could really fall for a girl like her. Oh well, he thought as he leaned his chair against the wall and picked up the fishing magazine again. There was a great article about hand tying trout lures and catching lunkers in the Sierras.

The corner store was not in a busy part of town being on the southern side of an industrial area, and so to attract attention to its many products and wares it had bright ads pasted to the windows, such as huge bottles of beer with bikini clad models on the beach.

Abby frowned as she approached the door. Standing to the side and pretending to read a newspaper was a young man about her age. He was clean shaven and his hair slicked back and trim, but something about him struck her as odd and a little out of place. He had a twinkle in his eye and he smiled at her with pure white teeth and an 'awe shucks' kind of look about him, and she softened here shield a little, but then she noticed that he had a scar that ran from his right cheek to his chin and his eyes did have a glint of anger on the edges in a way, and so she became edgy in her own way.

"How do Ma'am?" he said in a Texan drawl. "Sure is a fine day we're having."

"Yes," she replied with a forced smile as best she could, and made sure she could make it clear past him and through the front door before taking another step. "It is a fine day," and she kept her smile as she passed into the little store.

There was an old man with gray hair and glasses at the cash register and he nodded to her as she entered. The candy bars were up front where he could keep his eyes on them when the rascal kids came in looking for sweets. Candy was the number one shoplifted item in the world. Abby picked out an assortment of chocolate bars, ten in all, and then remembering Winston picked out three dark chocolate and almonds bars for him.

The clerk counted the bars. "That's thirteen," he said flatly.

"Yes, how much do I owe you?"

"Don't you want to buy another one? Or take one less?"

"Why would I want to do that?"

"Don't you know thirteen is an unlucky number?"

She laughed, "You're kidding me, right?"

The old man frowned. "I don't kid about things like that."

"Of all the things in the world you could worry about and you're worrying about me buying thirteen candy bars?"

"I like to look out for my customers."

"Well thank you for that." She thought for a moment, after all she was headed to an unknown part of Alaska and didn't know when she would get another chance, and then, "Well, I do like chocolate. I'll tell you what, I'll take ten more."

He smiled, "Now you're talking."

"Say," she leaned in towards him as she handed him a twenty dollar bill. "Have you ever seen that man that's standing out there?"

He took off his glasses and peered out the glass door. "Sure, he came a little while ago and bought a newspaper, the one he's reading now."

"Ever see him before today?"

"Nope, can't say that I have." He said as he turned towards her and put his eyeglasses back on.

"Why?"

She bit her lip. "No reason really." Women's intuition hell, that guy outside creeped the hell out of her.

He handed her the change and the bag of candy bars and smiled at her. "Enjoy that chocolate miss, biggest sale I ever made, for chocolate that is."

She took the bag and headed out the door, the bell on top jingling as she went out. The young man with the scar was holding the door for her and smiling at her. "Well how do again ma'am."

"Hello again," she said as she walked past him towards the street. Damned if the light wasn't red and traffic blocking her from crossing.

"Say miss..." he walked towards her, "I'm sorry to bother you but..."

Oh god, she thought, he's going to ask me for money. C'mon light, change, change.

"...well it's like this..." he continued, "I'm new in town you see..."

Okay, here we go, she thought.

"...I don't know anyone here, and I was just wondering if you might be able to maybe show me around a bit, you know maybe go out to dinner and a movie?"

Well I'll be damned, she thought as she looked sideways at him. He's asking me out on a date, a creepy date at that. Luckily, after many years of practice she was an expert at rejecting guys hitting on her. The light changed and the traffic stopped. "No thanks." She said simply and walked off the curb. You can't drag these kinds of things out she thought. When she was halfway across the road she looked back and he was staring at her, the awe shucks smile replaced by a stern look, and she started walking faster. She got to the gate house and whistled for Winston.

"There you are," he said, "that was quick."

She reached into the bag and pulled out his three candy bars and handed them to him, her hand was shaking a little. "There was some creepy guy outside the store, trying to talk to me and ask me out." She looked back across the street but the guy was gone.

"Oh yeah?" said Winston and he eyes narrowed. He looked across the street towards the store, but the sidewalk was empty as far as he could see. "Well he's gone now. Maybe he went back inside the store. You gotta be careful around here, Seattle is full of how should I say it, 'characters'."

"You're telling me."

"Don't worry Abby; you're safe inside this gate."

"Well, I better get back upstairs; we're just about ready to leave."

Jonah was at his desk working on his flight plan. He had a map spread out and with a red pen had drawn lines along the coastline to their destination in Alaska, eight hundred miles to the north.

"There's fog on the coast this morning, so we'll head inland for the first couple of hours and then

Cross over theses points of land later this afternoon. This is where we'll refuel." He pointed to a place on the map. "Harbor town, British Colombia."

"This is exciting. How do you know that there's fog on the coast?"

"Old Indian trick." He pointed to the binoculars on the desk.

"Very funny. Can I take a look?"

"Of course." He handed them to her.

"How do you focus it?"

"Here, let me show you, there's one eyepiece that rotates, and this lever focuses the whole thing."

While Abby was looking out the window, Jonah scanned the lab to see if there was anything he had missed. Every surface was gleaming and shining and clean, even the ceiling and the lights. And that's when he saw it, a little black spec in the space between the metal casing and the plastic lens of a long fluorescent light above the table with the pressure canisters.

"What the heck, how did that fly get in here?" He opened a drawer and took out a towel while keeping one eye on the black spec. Moving slowly and twirling the towel while holding one of the ends he fashioned a fly swatter. The light was ten feet in the air and he pulled a chair over and slowly stood on it, and then coiling his arm back he twacked the light and dislodged the fly. It fell on the floor next to the chair.

"Ha!" he exulted, "got him."

"What the heck?" Abby looked over at the sound.

"Damn fly in the lab, big sucker too, must be a horsefly," said Jonah. He bent down and was about to pick it up with the towel and flush it down the drain when he stopped. "What the heck is this?" he said, and opened a nearby drawer, pulled out some tweezers and used them to pick the fly off the ground, then walked over to a microscope and put the fly under the lens. He focused the microscope and studied the structure of the fly. It looked more like a wasp, with big eyes, and it looked like it was made of metal.

"This isn't a fly."

Abby came over from the window and stood next to Jonah.

"Take a look," he told her, and she sat down at the table and looked through the eyepiece, focusing with the knob.

It looked like a cross between a mosquito and a house fly.

"It's metal," she said. "And what looks like clear plastic for wings, and tiny camera lenses for eyes."

"We've been bugged," he said. "Again. There's no telling how long that thing's been there."

He quickly hooked up his camera to the microscope and took a couple of pictures.

"Now what?" she asked.

"I'll tell you what," he replied and picked the bug up with the tweezers and walked over to the stove sized incinerator, popped it inside, closed the door and flipped the switch. There was a popping sound like popcorn in a microwave and a little burst of flame through the dome window. Jonah opened the door to the incinerator and confirmed with his own eyes that the bugging device was now a tiny pile of ash.

"I've got to get in touch with Ross, and let him know there's been a security breach."

"Moldini?"

"I wouldn't put it past him, and the people he works for."

Jonah walked to the desk and picked up the phone, he clicked the on off button but it was silent.

"Now what the hell," he fumed.

"What?"

"No dial tone." He pulled his cell phone out of his pocket and tried dialing but he got a no service message. "Steel and concrete building, cell phones won't work."

There was an old intercom system by the door to the lab and he punched in the front desk.

"Penny does your phone work?"

"No Jonah, it went dead a couple of minutes ago, I was talking to a supplier and it just went blank."

Jonah punched in the intercom button for the gate. No answer. He grabbed the binoculars and went to the window and looked out, focusing on the gate. There was a police car at the gate, and a policeman was talking to Winston.

"Now I wonder what's going on out there?" wondered Jonah. "What a coincidence, I was going to call the police about the bug, and they're already here, almost like they knew about it in advance." He kept the binoculars on the gate house. "Old Winston doesn't look very happy about something."

"Can I take a look?"

Jonah handed her the binoculars and she brought them up to the window and focused. Winston had his back against the interior of the gate house she could just barely see him through the doorway. He was talking animatedly but his hands were at his side. The policeman wasn't saying a thing, just listening. She turned the knob to increase the magnification to see the policeman's face better. Her breath stuck in her throat when she saw the slick back hair, the scar that ran from his cheek bone to his chin. It was the guy from the store, the creep.

"I've seen that guy before; he's the one who was stalking me at the convenience store."

She kept the binoculars steady as the policeman brought a pistol out and levelled it at Winston. The barrel of the gun had a silencer on it, and white smoke puffed out of it and it bucked in his hand. Winston's face went blank as two red dots appeared on his forehead, and he fell to the ground out of sight. Abby dropped the binoculars and was paralysed; the binoculars clattering to the floor at her feet.

"What happened?" said Jonah, he could see Winston disappear out of sight but was too far away to see any details. Abby was pale and sobbing, and he picked up the binoculars and focused on the gate house. The policeman was pulling Winston into the gate house, he could see the bottoms of his feet as they disappeared past the door, and then the cop closed the door and looked at the lab, looked directly up into the window at Jonah who was looking at him with the binoculars. The cop sprinted towards the front of the building.

Jonah ran over to the intercom and punched the button for the front desk.

"C'mon Penny pick up, pick up!"

"Front desk, oh hi Jonah, I still can't get the phone to work. There's a policeman at the front door, something's happened, he's waving for me to let him in."

"Penny, listen to me, do not let him in!"

But there was silence on the other end, and he could hear her footsteps as she trotted towards the front door with her high heels clicking on the floor, and heard her greeting the cop. There were two muffled pops and then silence.

Jonah picked up the backpack with the OE57 canisters and went to the window where Abby still stood in shock.

"We gottta go," said Jonah and he pulled her away from the window and towards the door. He looked down the hallway towards the elevator, it was silent, the emergency stairwell was at one the end of the hall, and the fire escape on the outside of the building was on the other end. They ran towards the fire escape, Jonah pulled the fire alarm as they passed the elevator, and it began whooping with lights flashing.

The window opened quickly and they jumped out onto the fire escape landing, Jonah reclosed the window and they flew down the metal stairs, Jonah jumping halfway down each section and then helping Abby. Hugging the outer walls they crept around the building towards the front and stopped at the corner. Jonah's truck was parked near the entrance in full view of the lobby windows.

"Stay close to me and keep your eyes on the ground," he said.

He pulled her behind him to the edge of the first window and peered into the lobby using a sliver of glass for his view. The great room was empty, and then towards the entrance he saw the body sprawled on the ground.

"Let's go," he said and they continued walking slowing, he was searching the interior of the lobby as they walked and he was ready to backtrack and run with Abby if he saw so much as a shadow. The truck was just a few feet away now and he could clearly see Penny's crumpled body just inside the entrance next to a pool of dark blood. Abby saw also, her hand gripped his and he knew without looking back at her. A few more feet, he pulled her and they ran the rest of the distance. Abby went to the passenger's side and couldn't get the door open her hands were shaking so bad and sweating, her face contorted in fear. Jonah reached over and flung open the door and she scrambled in, and he turned the ignition and jammed the truck into reverse.

20.

Philip had pulled the police car up to the gate and started talking to the guard, who looked to be ex military, of the lazy type. He told him he had a search warrant for the premises and needed his cooperation.

There was some dried blood on the front of the blue uniform from the stupid cop that he got it from, and the guard asked about it, like it was any of his business.

The guard was ready to call on an intercom system and so Philip pulled out the pistol with the silencer on it and pointed it at his stomach.

"Don't do that," he told him. And the guy got belligerent, said he hadn't had a gun in his face since Iraq, as if Philip gave a rats ass about that. Normally an assassin would just put the bullet in his target as soon as he got the opportunity and the quicker the better, but Philip liked to see the fear in their faces, it made it more exciting, more fun, but this guy wasn't cooperating.

"What's a cop doing with a silencer on a gun?" he asked. Tried to tell Philip he was ex Green Beret or some crap, and so Philip put an end to the conversation with two quick bullets in the forehead.

He pulled the guy into the guard house but his damn big feet were getting in the way of closing the door so he had to leave it part way open and move on. The plan was for him to secure the building, eliminate any bystanders, assassinate the two scientists and cover for Monroe who would bring up the rear. They had already cut the phone and cable lines to the outside and had a jamming device pointed at the building to eliminate any cell phone signals. The people inside the building would be cut off from the outside world and Monroe could download all the computer data, confiscate the bacteria and they would destroy the building with dynamite on their way out.

A simple enough plan, except for one thing, Philip had done his homework and he knew that this Jonah character was somewhat of an outdoorsman and was known to carry a gun or two. That was something that needed to be addressed and quickly.

After he shot the guard and tried to close the door but was hindered by the big feet, Philip looked up at the third floor of the building and there, as clear as day was Jonah looking down at him with binoculars. He could see Abby with her hands by her mouth. He sprinted for the front door and waved for the secretary to let him in. She was very accommodating. Two more bullets in her forehead and he headed for the elevator. It was parked on the third floor, and not moving. He punched the elevator button to take that route away from them and waited till it arrived empty a moment later. He jammed a nearby chair leg into the opening and went to the stairway door. And then the fire alarm started going off. That was something they hadn't counted on. It was really loud, and now someone on the outside would hear it and call the fire department. He opened the door to the stairway slowly and once he could tell it was empty he started sprinting up the stairs to the third floor. He opened the door at the third floor landing ready to shoot or be shot. The hallway was empty and he crept up to the office with the 'Oil Eater' sign over it and peered in.

It was also empty, and he made his way through the office and into the lab, looking under tables and behind counters. He looked out the window at the parking lot and saw the truck burning rubber towards the gate, Monroe was crouched by the gate with the bag of dynamite and firing a pistol at the truck as it roared past him, crashed into the rear of the police car that was partially blocking the gate and kept going full speed down the highway towards the airport.

Philip raced down the stairway through the lobby past the dead secretary and out towards the gate. He passed Monroe who was hurrying towards the building.

"I'm going after them! You're on your own!" he shouted and jumped into the police car, turned on the siren, slammed it into reverse and nearly broke the transmission cramming it into drive while still speeding backwards and with tires smoking and screaming took off after the truck.

Monroe walked steadily towards the building, and then began running as he heard the fire truck sirens in the distance. "Ten minutes," he told himself. "Download the data, blow the building and escape and you'll never have to work again."

21.

Jonah looked in the rear view mirror as he sped away from the lab, and then slowed down to the speed level so he wouldn't attract attention. What the heck just happened, he wondered. My God they shot Winston and Penny; he could see her crumpled body by the front door as they drove past towards the gate. And who was the guy shooting at them by the gate house? There was the cop, and the other guy, no telling how many others there were. One thing was certain though, they were after them for the OE 57 and there was nothing that they wouldn't do to get it.

Abby was sobbing with her head in her hands buried in her lap. It was heartbreaking, but he needed to get them away from here fast.

The airport was five minutes away and the plane was loaded and ready to go. He swerved in between traffic and then up ahead saw the red light. He was stuck in the right lane with nowhere to go, about five cars back from the light. He heard the sound of fire engines in the distance, the distinctive honk of the big horn as they weaved through the traffic. The light stayed red in front of him, and now he knew why. The fire and police had a computer chip so that when they were coming to a light while in an emergency, the signal light would stay green for them. The big fire truck raced through the intersection from the right, took the turn and sped off down the road towards the lab a few blocks back. Now there was the sound of police cars, he could tell the higher pitched sound, and he looked in the rear view mirror and saw the lights from a police car a couple of blocks back and headed their way. The light was still red damn it and he was blocked in and he spun the wheel to the right and drove onto sidewalk and turned at the corner and floored it down the road towards the airport, a car sideswiped him or he sideswiped it and the other car spun out of control in the middle of the road behind them, horns were honking right and left and he wrestled with the steering wheel of the truck. He could see the control tower just a half mile away and he pushed the accelerator to the floorboard and the truck was going over eighty, and he had to ease on the brake so he wouldn't skid out of control to make the turn into the private plane parking area, in the rear view mirror he could see the flashing lights of the police car gaining on them.

They pulled in next to the locked gate and abandoned the truck, Jonah punched in the code on the gate lock and they ran to his plane. He pulled the chocks off the wheels and jumped into the plane and started the engine.

"Where are we going Jonah?" asked Abby as she put on her seatbelt. Her eyes were red and swollen from crying.

"Somewhere far away from here," said Jonah, "hang on 'cause here we go."

The plane's engine and propeller turned over with a chuga chug and then roared to life. He quickly scanned the gauges, full tank, oil pressure fine, he moved the controls and the stick up and down, worked the flaps up and down, with his head on a swivel watching the wings and the road next to the hanger.

The police car raced around the bend at eighty miles an hour with no lights or siren, and came skidding into the parking lot in a cloud of dust. He could see the man dressed in the police uniform get out with a long rifle and run towards the fence.

Jonah gunned the engine and headed towards the runway.

There were two other small planes waiting in line to use the runway, he'd have to cut in front of them. Through the windshield he could see what the little planes were waiting for. A large jet airliner was easing down from the sky and about a mile away.

The back window shattered with a sudden terrifying crash of broken glass as though struck with a hammer. The bullet ricocheted up and through the top of the roof leaving a can sized opening with jagged edges.

"Keep your head down!" Shouted Jonah, and pushed Abby towards the floor of the passenger seat.

He began to weave the plane down the tarmac, and another bullet bounced off the cabin with a clap.

The airliner was landing now in front of them as they raced towards the runway. The big jet airplane bounced a bit as the wheels touched the asphalt and the rubber smoked with friction as the weight of the jet settled on the landing gear and it roared past them to the right.

Jonah jerked the steering wheel and skidded around the two other planes and headed off down the runway after the jet. The people in the other planes looked over as they passed by with shock on their faces.

"Sorry," muttered Jonah.

His radio crackled, it was the tower.

"Small plane, small plane on runway two, stop your engine, repeat stop your engine!"

Jonah rammed the throttle forward and the plane rapidly accelerated and began to gain on the jet ahead.

"This might be close," muttered Jonah.

Another bullet tore through the cabin and went straight through the radio, sparks were flying and some smoke was streaming out of the dash.

The airspeed gauge read ninety five miles per hour, and he pulled back on the stick ever so slightly and the plane was free from the earth.

The tail of the jet thirty feet in height was looming in front of them and fast approaching, with his airspeed passing one hundred he pulled back on the stick and held his breath as they flew over the jet.

The pilots in the cockpit of the jet heard the sudden roar above them and then saw the plane pass over head just a few feet above them and they instinctively ducked.

"Son of a bitch!" shouted the captain. "I'm gonna put that guy on report!"

"Sorry guys," Jonah said as he waved his wings and banked away from the runway.

The plane bucked and bumped as it rose steadily into the clear sky.

He scanned the sky for more aircraft as he headed for the ocean. A line of fog was marching in from the west about a mile out. He looked back towards the hanger where the gunman fired from, but it was very small and disappearing in the distance.

"We're safe for now," said Jonah. "You can get up."

The radio was still smoking and he reached under his seat and brought out a little fire extinguisher. He pointed the nozzle and gave the radio it a couple of short blasts and the smoke disappeared. Five hundred feet in the air and cruising at one hundred twenty miles an hour, Abby buckled back into her seat and smoothed her hair back. Tears were streaming down her face and she wiped them with her hand.

"What are we going to do now?"

"I don't know," said Jonah. "But one thing's for certain, we need to get away from this area quick. I don't know who is after us; it could be one guy, or a hundred. I don't exactly know who's involved, but I do know what they're after." He pointed his thumb towards the rear seats. "Our little creation."

Abby put her head in her hands and sobbed. "It's all my fault. If I wouldn't have approached you with my big idea none of this would have happened."

"Nonsense, someone else would have come up with that combo sooner or later. We should have been more careful. Somehow, someone planted that bug and found out everything we'd been doing. There could have been multiple bugs for all we know. When we found the fly on the wall device in the office, they knew their surveillance was finished and they came in with guns blazing."

"Poor Winton, and Penny. She was so sweet."

"Yeah poor Winton, he didn't deserve that. My good old fishing buddy. Those bastards will get what's coming to them; I'll make sure of it. They want this oil eating bacteria? I'll give it to 'em. I'll put it in every well in the world. Dry up every drop."

It was nearly a hundred miles to the coast and he headed straight for it.

In less than an hour they were over the ocean and headed for the fog bank that straddled the coastline. He turned the aircraft north and flew along the edge of the grey mist.

"Where are we going?" She asked.

"British Columbia. About five hundred miles north of here there's a giant wilderness area with lakes and waterways, a lot of places inaccessible without a plane. I know a couple of spots. We'll fly in under the radar, and hide out for a couple of days till we find out what's going on. I don't think that was a cop but we can't take any chances."

"If it was a bad cop we don't know if he was working alone right?"

"That's right," he said. "There's no way we can go to the police yet, can't let anyone else get involved and maybe get them hurt. These people are ruthless. I know Moldini is involved, it's his people, and maybe others."

22.

The ocean below was rippled with light winds from the fog, and a fishing boat was headed back to port, it's white wake in an expanding vee trailing behind it.

A small helicopter was moving quickly along the coast and at water level well ahead of them.

"Check out that helicopter," he said as he pointed down to it. "He's going about one fifty. Our top speed is only around one thirty with the pontoons."

"How much farther to the border?"

"About twenty minutes. As soon as that helicopter gets farther ahead we'll dip down to a little under a hundred feet so we're undetected."

"There's radar at the border?"

"Loaded. This whole area is bustling with military and commercial radar."

They flew in silence with only the sound of the wind blowing through the cabin and the steady rumble of the engine. The helicopter was two miles ahead now, and it started to rise to their level. It seemed to be getting larger, and closer. It's was hovering, the pilots side facing towards them.

"What's this now?" said Jonah with worry in his voice.

They were closing rapidly now and Jonah maneuvered the plane to the left and away from the path near the copter.

"This isn't good," he said as the pilots' side window in the helicopter opened and a rifle muzzle appeared, the metal barrel shining in the sunlight.

He banked hard left as smoke puffed from the muzzle and banked again hard right. The bullet missed and Jonah plunged the airplane into a dive towards the water. The air was screaming along the wings, he looked in the rear-view mirror and Abby turned in her seat to see the helicopter right on their tail. There was only the pilot, and it looked like the same gunman, the policeman from the building and the airport, with short cropped hair, and intense face.

"He's too fast, we'll never outrun him in this tin can," shouted Jonah over the wind.

He banked hard left again and straight into the fog bank. The airplane screamed in its dive towards the water and at fifty feet he pulled back on the stick. The plane shuddered with stress.

"C'mon baby," pleaded Jonah.

Abby held onto the seat, her knuckles turning white as the water came into view.

The plane levelled out just a few feet from the water. The helicopter was still close behind.

Jonah tried banking left and then right to get some space between them and the copter. If only he could get thirty feet away he could lose it, but the copter stayed just close enough.

Suddenly up ahead a large fishing boat, a trawler was in their path. Jonah banked hard left, the helicopter banked hard right both missing the trawler by inches. The fishermen topside flung themselves to the deck covering their heads as the two aircraft roared overhead.

"Got him," said Jonah as he kept his turn, and then straightened out and pulled up the flaps cutting his airspeed. "Get ready to land," he shouted to Abby. She put her head between her knees and folded her hands over her hair.

The pontoons bounced on the water once, twice and then held. Jonah cut the engine and the plane came to a slow stop on the ocean. The water lapped over the pontoons and the plane turned into the slight breeze. It was cold in the fog and quiet. Off in the distance they could hear the pop pop pop of the helicopter rotor as it zigzagged in circles trying to find them.

Abby and Jonah held their breath as the thick fog closed around them. The sound of the helicopter slowly faded away, and soon it was quiet.

They sat there for at least five minutes before either one spoke.

Finally Abby let out a sigh of relief. "Nice landing," she said.

"Yeah," Jonah let out his own sigh. "Lucky thing for us that boat showed up. Did you get a look at the pilot in the helicopter."

"The same guy at the research facility, and the airport."

"That's what I thought too. He must have commandeered that helicopter, it's used for tours of the city and Mount Rainier, I know the company. They have a fleet at the airport gassed up and ready to go."

Off in the distance they heard the mournful sound of a fog horn. They listened intently and a minute later the fog horn bellowed again.

"Sounds like its getting farther away," she said.

"Agreed."

The third bellow confirmed their assumption.

"That's a big foghorn, must be a big ship, maybe a tanker nearby. We'd better wait till the fog lifts a bit. I've had too many close calls for one day. "

He looked at his watch, nine thirty in the morning. A few black and white Sea birds were floating nearby. They were also grounded due to the fog.

"We could probably get some fishing in," said Jonah, and then he thought of Winton and when he lowered his head Abby put her hand on his shoulder in comfort. Within an hour the heat from mid morning sun had broken the fog into clumps and they could see hundreds of yards in all directions.

"Time to go," said Jonah and he cranked the engine. The takeoff was rough and the little plane bounced and sloshed through the swells and then broke free from the water and was airborne again. They rose through the remaining fog and flew along the tops of the wispy cloud. The coast was still obscured by the fog and he flew straight north for an hour till they were well into Canadian airspace, and then turned towards the land. They flew low over the top side of Vancouver Island and then the Johnstone straits, and then turned north again. The land below was forest as far as the eye could see and they flew on just over the treetops. Now and then they would pass over logging operations, and lakes and streams. Soon the logging roads became fewer and the lakes and streams increased in number.

"God's country," said Jonah.

Abby was in awe, she had never seen such a wide expanse of wilderness.

"This is all Indian land set aside for the tribes," continued Jonah. "The Cree, and the Chippewa, they roamed this land for thousands of years. There's still a few scattered here and there. This is Huaskin Lake, great fishing. But not today."

He turned east again and they flew between two towering mountains. Up and over a ridge and they were headed straight for a little lake at the base of one of the peaks. There was a small island at the southern portion and he circled it and scanned the shoreline. The lake was two thousand feet at its widest and a thousand at its narrowest and was shaped like a Scottish bagpipe. "This is it," said Jonah.

"Is there enough room to land?"

"Easy."

Abby checked her buckle and gripped the seat again as Jonah circled and then headed into the wind and throttled back. They glided down and touched down on the still and cold lake as the sun was setting in the West. Jonah kept the props turning and maneuvered to the little island, and as they got closer he turned off the engine and they eased towards the shoreline.

There was a small round bay just big enough for the wingspan of the plane and they headed in that direction. He grabbed the paddle and rope from the rear of the plane and jumped out onto the pontoon and brought them closer to the beach. It was strewn with small rounded pebbles and driftwood and he jumped into the shallow water and tied the plane to a nearby log.

The pontoons rested gently on the shallow bottom. The round little island was about a hundred feet across and two hundred yards from the shore. Abby climbed onto the pontoon under her door, and made her way along it to the beach. She reached out to the metal cowling that covered the engine for balance, it was hot and she pulled her hand back and tiptoed along the pontoon, under the still prop and hopped onto the shore.

She looked at the towering trees that covered the island. "So this is home?"

"For a while," said Jonah. "It's been years since I've been here. It's quiet, secluded. The fishing is not that great, so we shouldn't see any other people, no real reason to fly up here. We just have to watch out for Bears."

"Bears?"

"Oh yeah. Grizzly bears, and Black bears. They come down out of the mountains about this time of year right before the salmon spawn."

"But isn't this island far enough out to keep them away?"

"For hunters yes, for bears no. They're great swimmers, so we'll have to be on our toes. There's also wolves and mountain lions, they won't swim out here, but a bear could."

Jonah jumped back onto the pontoon and reached into the cockpit and pulled out a holstered handgun. He checked the chamber of the handgun and strapped the gun in the holster to his waist. Then he reached back in and pulled out a rifle and checked its chamber.

"You ever use one of these?"

23.

Philip Weintraub circled the helicopter in the dense fog. Damn that fishing boat. He slammed his fist into the dashboard and blood welled on his knuckles. He zigzagged back and forth in the direction that the plane had headed after their near collision with the boat. Nothing.

He headed straight north again and climbed high out of the cloud and searched the sky.

Anything could have happened, they could have crashed, or landed safe in the water, or were at this moment flying through the fog bank. They were headed north when he started tailing them that was for sure. This Jonah dude must have some sort of plan, some safe haven he was heading for. If they were still flying in the fog they wouldn't be too far away, and if they landed they'd have to take off again, and if they'd crashed they'd either call for a rescue, or he'd read about it in the obituaries.

Philip thought quickly and made up his mind. The copter shot forward and was soon going at full speed north. Twenty minutes of flying left him seventy miles north of the position where he'd lost the plane. He flew along the coast and found a secluded hilltop on a rugged cliff above the ocean and landed. The rotors slowed and the whine of the jet engine wound down and he climbed out of the cockpit with his binoculars.

The fog was lifting somewhat in the midmorning sun, and he scanned the horizon.

At two hundred miles per hour the helicopter would have doubled the slow bush planes distance, and since he'd flown for twenty minutes they would be ten minutes behind. He searched intently in a hundred eighty degree circle towards the south and west.

Ten minutes came and went, then twenty and then half an hour had passed since he landed. Nothing. He thought he saw a plane at one point, but it turned out to be a flock of birds far out on the horizon. If they'd landed in the water it could be any time in the distant future that they could take off and elude him unless he stayed here. They also could have gone back in the opposite direction to throw him off the trail. That's what I would do, he thought. So the Fox had been out foxed. The sinking realization of this made his stomach turn. It was a simple job; the security was minimal, not like some of his targets in the past.

It was his partner. Monroe had gotten in the way. He was old, slow. Another reason why I like to work alone, he thought. Why did I let them talk me into it? Never again he swore.

That sinking feeling of failure crept into the back of his mind, and he knew if he didn't score this hit, he would never get another job again. He would be on the hit list. He scanned the horizon for another twenty minutes. It had now been over an hour since he lost the plane in the fog. Plan B he thought. He stripped off the police uniform and was now down to surf shorts and tee shirt, cradled the mirror sunglasses on his nose and surveyed the inland.

He needed transportation, and needed to get away from this helicopter quick. There over a nearby hill was a dirt road that led to level farmland. Some type of crop was being grown there, it looked like pumpkins or squash. Where there was farmland there would be a farm, and a farmer with a truck.

He wiped down all the controls that he'd touched, piled the uniform in a little ball and brought it with him. He'd bury it in a hole on the way. He wished he could torch the helicopter but it would bring too much attention too quickly. All he needed to do now was just get away, and find a place to blend in. It would be easy to blend in here in Canada. He'd get to the nearest town and make some calls, monitor the news. Somewhere there was a plane all shot to hell, and someone would know about it. It wasn't a normal thing to have a bush plane with bullet holes in it, and he was sure he'd blown out a couple of the windows, and when they landed at a harbor or dock for gas someone would say something. He wasn't the only one looking for that plane, or for this helicopter for that matter. He would need to get a police scanner right away and monitor the airwaves.   He grabbed the rifle from the copter and headed down the hill towards the farm.

24.

"Didn't you say the fishing was no good here?"

The line screamed from his reel and the pole was bent in half and Jonah struggled to reply.

"Well," he started, and had to quickly ease off the drag. "Last time I was here it wasn't." He got the pole under control as the line cut sideways through the water. A few yards away a large trout lunged into the air contorting its body and tail in an airborne ballet and splashed back into the lake. Jonah cranked the handle of the reel and got some line back before it screamed again and the fish was off and running. Two more jumps and one more half hearted scream of the line and the fish was done for. Jonah led it exhausted to the bank of the island and gently put his fingers into its gills and lifted it out. He held it at arm's length and estimated its weight. "Eight pounds," he said finally.

"Is that good?"

"That's excellent. But since we have enough already, this one gets to go home." He eased the treble hook out of its mouth and submerged it in the water, and after a moment to let it right itself he let it go. The fish slowly swam away and then quickly darted into the deep water. "Well that was exciting. I didn't think I was going to land that one. What do you say we call it a day. I caught a couple, you caught a couple. Now we can eat lunch."

"And not any cold peanut butter and jelly sandwiches," She sighed with relief.

Last night after landing they opened his food store that he kept on board and had PB&J sandwiches and juice with a shot of rum. He folded the aircraft seats down and laid down the little futons that he kept in the back. A piece of plastic was cut in half and taped to the hole in the ceiling and the broken back windshield. It was chilly and uncomfortable, but after their harrowing day had a feeling of relief at being alive.

He reached down into the cold water and pulled out the stringer that held the fish. Five rainbow trout were lifeless on the line. A flat black rock served as a cutting board and he brought out his hunting knife and began cleaning and scaling the fish. The head and guts went into the lake to feed the crabs and small fish, and he washed each one in the clear water and laid them back on the rock and covered them with a towel.

Abby stood nearby admiring his work; he was very precise with the knife. "You should have been a surgeon."

He went back to the plane and got a small shovel from the back. "Now I'm going to show you an old Indian trick."

He found a level clearing nearby and dug two small holes side by side. Each hole was about the size of a mailbox and only a few inches apart. Once the dirt was cleared out he reached into one of the holes and with his hand dug a little tunnel between them at the bottom.

"This is a Dakota fire pit," he explained. "One of the holes has the fire and the other acts as the vent."

He began stuffing bark and wood into one of the holes. One of the keys to this fire is using the driest material you can find. When he was finally satisfied with the arrangement of the wood, he brought out a lighter from his pocket and lit the tinder bark. Flames shot quickly down the hole, and a small compact column of smoke rose like a rope from it.

"You see once the fire gets going, the heat rises straight up and draws the air from the vent next to it into the bottom of the fire. It's a really efficient way to manage a cooking fire. The Dakota Indians used this method so the fire wouldn't get out of control, spread out in the wind and burn down the forest. And since you don't need much wood to make a hot fire you have very little smoke. Go ahead put your hand right next to the hole."

She crouched down and felt the ground. "It's cold."

"Now hold your hand up here." He held his hand four feet above the hole, and she followed.

"Hot, very hot." And she withdrew her hand, blowing on it.

"You rig a tripod of green wood high over the

pit and then you can hang a pot of stew over the heat and cook it all day long." He began to place large rocks around the hole. "But what we're going to do is use it like a stove and fry up some fresh trout."

He went back to the plane and retrieved a large cast iron frying pan and spatula, plates forks and spices and began frying up the fish. The aroma of the crackling pan mixed with the pine scent of the forest and filled the air.

Abby sat on a rock and watched. "How much time do you spend up here, flying around and camping in the woods?"

"Every chance I get. It's funny, me and my Dad used to do a lot of hiking to get to a good fishing spot, and then one summer we took a tour with a guide up in Alaska. He had this little pipsqueak of a plane, a four seat Piper cub that he modified with pontoons and we could barely fit ourselves and our gear in. We flew into the wilderness and landed on this little lake in the middle of nowhere. Our guide had built a little cabin in the woods one summer all by himself with a chainsaw using the pine trees around the lake. No permit, no government oversight, no one even knew or cared that he built it or that we were there, and we fished for a week from the shore and scored big time, trout and pike and walleye, and at the end I didn't want to leave. To me it was a paradise, the pinnacle of freedom, flying deep into the wilderness and living off the land. That was it for me. I was seventeen."

Jonah opened a can of corn and placed it on one of the rocks next to the fire pit. Abby was still curious. "So how many days a year do you camp? You seem to know how live pretty comfortably out here."

"Oh, just about every weekend. I don't know, maybe a hundred days a year."

"What? That's a lot. Why so much?"

"I don't know, part of it is the quiet, there's no cars or trucks, no people, no TV, internet, no opinions, no one telling you what they think or why they think it, or anyone telling you what to do, or how to do it, what you see is what you get. This is pure reality, pure nature, and you might think this is kind of corny but I think I come up here a lot to get closer to our creator. I call it reality TV without the TV."

He turned the fish in the iron pan with a metal spatula and there was a hiss from the oil and steam rising.

He continued. "When I was growing up we would go to church every Sunday, and it was usually stinking hot inside, no wind, just a little fan, and I remember looking out the window most of the time as the preacher preached about God and spirit and righteous living, and I remember looking out the window and thinking, out there is spirit, and I'd look around at everyone listening to the words and think that sure there is spirit inside everyone it's true as the bible says, but when you look at the blue sky and clouds, and green trees, and rivers and streams, now that is alive and moving, and that is a spirit you can see with your eyes. You can see it and feel it, and its mind boggling, and you can talk all you want about the greatness of God till you're blue in the face, but all you have to do is take a walk through a forest to really feel it." He broke a twig and tossed the pieces into the fire pit. "I guess this is kind of like going to church for me."

There was silence and he waited for a reaction from her. The wind gently rustled the tops of the pines and a trout jumped out on the lake, the circles of the splash spreading out on the otherwise glass smooth surface. Off in the far distance a moose called out, the sound of it bounding through the ravines.

Finally she replied slowly at first, unsure whether she should reveal this much about herself.

"I guess I'm a little embarrassed to say it but I'm sort of an agnostic."

"A what?"

"You know what I mean."

"Sorry, I just haven't met one in long time. The phrase was coined by Thomas Huxley in Eighteen Sixty Nine and I quote, 'follow your reason as far as it will take you without regard to any other consideration, but don't pretend that conclusions are certain that cannot be demonstrated'. It was a frontal attack on the basic principal of faith, in believing in something you can't see."

"Well that's where I'm at for good or bad.

When I was ten my Mom got cancer and it lingered forever it seemed, and on her last day she lay there unconscious and I overheard my Dad praying to God to spare her. It didn't help."

"I'm sorry."

"My Dad was pretty disappointed when I told him; I had to explain the word to him. I was about fourteen when I made up my mind. He blamed it on my fixation with science. I don't know why I gravitated towards it, but once I had a basic framework of knowledge I started asking my own questions. I was fascinated by how you could study things with microscopes, and looked at everything I could find. The microscopes I used got bigger and bigger, and I dug deeper and deeper into cell structure and then I got to the structure of atoms and I remember being astounded. I'd watch the stars at night in the backyard and think about how small an atom is and how big the universe is..."

"But your name is Abby. Isn't that part of a church?"

Pretty funny don't you think?"

"Ironic, not funny."

My Dad passed when I was sixteen, and then I lived in a few foster homes until I graduated from high school two years early and I worked my way through college and pre med."

"Looks like we're both alone," said Abby.

He smiled. "You know that's not true Abby. No one is ever alone, even when there's no one around."

The moment came and went and they found themselves sitting in silence listening to the world around them with nothing left to say on the matter, and a certain kind of comfort settled within them.

25.

A thousand pounds of Grizzly bear lumbered down the mountain towards the lake below. It was mid morning and the sun was shining long beams of light through the forest.

The big old bear hunched back on his hind legs and lifted his massive frame in the air, and stood straight up with his front legs with its giant paws and black claws hanging down at his side for balance. His dark brown fur with points of silver on the tips was thick and stank to the high heavens, and swarms of flies followed him every step of his journey. He sniffed the air while turning his head in a semi circle from right to left and back again, his nostrils flaring with each big whiff.

Something was different; there was a scent in the air that had his attention. For the past couple of days he'd been feasting on blackberries in the high fields. And then this morning he'd battled a pack of wolves over a moose carcass that the pack had brought down that night. He'd come across the kill just after dawn. He could smell fresh blood meat from far away, and had come rumbling across and down the valley towards it. He approached slowly as the wolves tore into the flesh of the moose lying dead and still on the ground.   They growled and snapped at one another as they gorged themselves. And then they saw him coming and barked and growled as he approached. Rage filled his mind. He was hungry and they would not share. He growled as loud as he could and burled his body to make it seem as big as possible and false charged them snarling his fangs, but they didn't budge from the carcass. They ripped into it with renewed fervor and kept their wary eyes on him.

He sniffed the air and his stomach churned with hunger and he charged into the pack to get at the meat. Normally a bear this size could take on a pack of four or five wolves, but this pack had ten and that made the matter much worse.

They broke away from the carcass as he charged and they all lunged at him and surrounded him. He sat on his rear end and wheeled with his paws swatting at them as they flew around him with their razor sharp teeth flashing in the sun. They were small and quick, and he was big and slow. If he could only catch them he could crush them but they stayed just out of his reach and nipped at him as they ran around him in circles. He got lucky and wacked a couple of them with his big paws, and they yelped away with pain, but soon returned to the fray.

He was way outnumbered and after a couple of wolves got in some quick bites on his back, he leaped into the air and rumbled away from the carcass with the pack nipping at his back heels as he ran and left them with their spoil.

Now he was hungry and more than ever in the mood for meat and he began to make his way down the mountain, down to the rivers and the streams below in search of fish.

It was late summer and his instincts told him to head down the mountain where the fish would be running. And so he plodded along for awhile, and stood on his hind legs again sniffing the air like a big dog, a very, very big and bad tempered dog. He was big enough that if anything got in his way he smashed it, except for a pack of wolves that is.

There were only two things that he was really afraid of, one was bees, they stung his nose and made his eyes water till he couldn't see.

He loved honey but hated bees and ran from them, they were too hard to catch and smash. The other thing he hated was man. He loved the food they had in their cabins and cars, but he hated the sting of their guns, it was a bigger sting than the bee and he avoided them whenever he could. Right now though he was hungry, and he fairly galloped down the hill towards the strange scent.

He followed his nose and it led him to the little lake in the shadow of the mountain. He sniffed the air again, and was now certain of the direction. The smell of the food was coming from the island across the water. The unnatural shape of the plane on the island was unfamiliar to him, but he was smart enough to know it meant man.

He shuffled on his front feet from side to side unsure if he should keep going forward, but in the end his rumbling stomach took control of his brain and he plodded into the water and began swimming, his giant body under water with just his head and nose above the surface, plowing forward, propelled by four giant paws doing the doggie paddle in unison. The bear's nose plowed through the water like a snorkel and the vee from his wake spread across the otherwise calm surface. His front paws found the sloping cobblestone bank of the island and he pulled himself out of the water and shook his frame like a giant dog. He padded slowly along the shoreline towards the plane sniffing the air as he went.

Abby saw him first and jumped to her feet, her plate with the half eaten fish clattering to the ground, her face sheet white, unable to bring a sound to her lips, breath frozen in her lungs.

Jonah was startled and his first thought was that she swallowed a fish bone and was choking and he should get ready to perform a Heimlich maneuver. Then the bear growled low in the distance and he followed her eyes to see the source of her terror. The plane was in between them and the bear, and it plodded steadily towards it. Jonah reached down for the gun in the holster and made sure it was still there. It was the biggest bear he'd ever seen or heard about. Grizzlies were feared by most of the other creatures in the forest. Black bears would run for the hills or climb the nearest tree if they spotted a Grizzly as they were no match for the sheer size and strength. Pack wolves would only battle a Grizzly if their numbers were overwhelming, and usually only to defend a meal they already had on the ground.

The average weight of full grown male Grizzly was anywhere from four hundred to eight hundred pounds.

Jonah tried to estimate this bears weight as it came closer to the plane, warily now.

"It's a male, and he looks like he's over a thousand pounds, easy," he said as he pulled the pistol out of the holster. He looked down at the gun in his hand and grimaced. This little pea shooter would only make the bear mad. He needed the rifle and it was propped against a tree next to the plane. "I want you to slowly move behind me Abby. Very slowly," he whispered as he rose to his feet.

As if floating in a dream she looked over at him and tried to move her feet that were stuck in quicksand, her whole body was numb and buzzing. "That's it," he reassured her. "Now slow as you can I want you to make your way into the forest behind us, whatever you do don't run or cry out. Go slow. Find a nice tree in the middle of the island and get at least fifteen feet in the air. I'm going to try to distract him and chase him away and back into the water." He paused for the words to sink in, "Okay?"

He turned his head so he could see her in the corner of his eye. She was slowly nodding and then turned and started moving towards the forest.

The bear was sniffing the plane now and he put his front paws on a pontoon and craned his head towards the open window in the cockpit.

The smoke from the fire had made its way to the plane and gathered in the cabin with a glorious smell from the oil of the frying fish. Curious as a bear normally is, he started to climb onto the pontoon with his back legs so he could get a better look and stick his nose into the window.

With his front paws balancing safely on the cowling of the plane, he put his right back paw on the pontoon, and stood straight up. The full weight of the beast went onto the front of the pontoon and the nose of the aluminum pontoon bent with a groan of twisting metal.

The bear lost his balance and bounded off the plane twisting his giant body with a strange grace and with all four paws on ground looked with suspicion at the plane. Still the smell of the fish was luring him forward and he heeded its siren call. The rumbling in his stomach was increasing as the smells unleashed a torrent of hunger juices. Saliva dripped from his mouth as he made his way around the nose of the plane towards the wisp of smoke coming from the ground.

Jonah had made his way towards the forest and was crouched behind a tree. The bear was going to head towards the fish at the fire and nothing could stop it.

"I'll let him get to the fish, he'll be distracted as he eats," thought Jonah. "And then I'll circle around to the rifle."

The Grizzly lumbered towards the fire. He stopped suddenly and sniffed the air. Bears have an incredible sense of smell, and this bear with a nose as big as a mailbox was particularly adept. The scent coming from the trees nearby was no scent of fish; it was the scent of an animal, with skin and hair and sweat. He eyed the tree line carefully, but the smell of the fish finally overwhelmed him and he spied the bones and half eaten carcasses on the ground ahead and half galloped the remainder of the way.

While the bear feasted on the trout, Jonah crept silently from tree to tree towards the plane. He had just a couple of tree left between himself and the rifle. The bear had slurped off the ground the remainder of the fish and was sniffing around for more. The little tidbits had barely whetted his appetite, and only increased his need for more of the same. He sniffed the ground around the fire and then widened his circle of sniffing and looked around the campsite. And then he spotted Jonah sliding between two trees. The bear stiffened in alarm, snarled and whirled to face his attacker, and then let out a great roar. His eyes filled with rage, his fur standing on end and he lunged forward with menace in a bluff charge, and stood still, his mouth open, teeth and fangs bared, slobber flowing from his chin.

Jonah also stood still and looked not at the bear's eyes but at his paws. He reached over slowly and grabbed the rifle and quickly checked the camber and locked it off. A bear can run over thirty miles an hour in short bursts, and Jonah estimated that this bear could travel the fifty yards that separated them in about three seconds. He didn't want to kill the bear, but he knew he would have no choice if it charged him.

A mortally wounded bear, especially one this large could survive long enough to tear him apart. He had one bullet in the chamber and ten in the magazine. If he turned and ran the bear could easily catch him, so he stood his ground and aimed the weapon. The bear came slowly at him, not charging but growling as it approached.

"I'll give him one chance," thought Jonah. "And then it's over for the big guy if he doesn't leave."

Being in the wilderness so often he'd naturally come into contact with bears quite a few times. They were usually attracted to the smell of his fish, and if he fired a warning shot they'd leave the area. Most of the bears he'd seen were the smaller black bears that were easily frightened away. In all his time in the wild he'd only seen one Grizzly bear, and that one had been less than half the size of this monster.

He aimed just above the bears head and squeezed off a shot. As the bullet was leaving the muzzle, the bear lifted his head, and the bullet ripped through his ear. The blast of the gun echoing through the forest, and the sudden sharp pain of his ear shocked the bear and he turned in his tracks and ran away. He smashed through the campfire and headed down the shoreline away from the danger, crashed into the water and swam for the other shore. Jonah ran to the plane and got out the binoculars and focused on the bears head. He could see that the right ear was ragged from where the bullet had torn the tip of it, and unlike the other ear which was perfectly round; this ear had a distinct vee in it.

"So be it," thought Jonah. "That big boy will be alright. I hope that wound makes him think twice before he tries to raid another campsite." He continued to watch the bear as it swam away and it wasn't long before it reached the other side and bounded into the forest. And then Jonah walked into the woods to find Abby. He found her on the other side of the island high up in a pine tree, and he yelled up at her. "I said at least fifteen feet in the air, not fifty!"

Her voice was shaking. "I wasn't taking any chances." She was five stories in the air. "Is it dead, did you kill it?"

"Naw I just chased it away."

"Are you kidding me?" she yelled. "Won't it just come back?"

"Not likely."

Her eyes flashed anger, but her voice trembled. "How can you be so sure?"

"Trust me."

"I don't know." She was holding tight to the tree with her arms wrapped around the trunk, and her feet snug on the branches. It was safe up here. She looked around and finally realized just how high she had climbed. It was all a blur now, running through the forest and hearing the bear roar behind her at the lake, she actually thought it was chasing her, and then she spotted this pine tree with the limbs near the ground and fairly shot up the trunk till her arms couldn't move another inch. It's a lot easier to climb up a tree than down it, as she soon found out, and as she made her way to the ground she nearly slipped more than once. The fear of the bear was replaced with the fear of falling, and by the time she touched her feet on the ground her hands and arms were covered with scratches.

She sat on the ground for a moment to catch her breath and wipe away a tear. He sat next to her in silence and cradled the rifle on his lap.

"That was a little bit scary," she said finally.

He nodded. "I had a teddy bear when I was a kid, what about you?"

She wiped away another tear and laughed. "Yes."

"I called mine Barry. Barry the bear, I took him with me everywhere. Did yours have a name?"

She sighed and smiled, and the tension drained out of her. "Harry. Harry the bear Harry I'd say and drag him around the house, tucked in every night with Harry the bear Harry. That bear that came out of the lake was a lot bigger than my Harry though."

"He was a big one alright. You should have seen his face when I shot the rifle at him."

Jonah told her all the details about how he snuck between the trees trying to get to the rifle and when the bear spotted him it charged.

"I just wanted to scare the big guy away, and I was ready to put him down if I had to. He lifted his head at the last moment and the bullet went right through his ear. He turned tail and ran as fast as he could. He's probably still running."

"I hope he tells all his friends to stay away too."

"Well I think a bear that big probably chased away all the other bears a long time ago. We should be okay now, but I'm taking any chances, this rifle will stay close by from now on." He patted the wooden stock and got to his feet and helped her up. "Let's go see if we can fix that radio."

In the height of the excitement of a thousand pound bear threatening mortal destruction Jonah did not notice the pontoon that it had stood on and crushed. Jonah and Abby stood looking down at the twisted metal of the pontoon. There were gaping holes and sharp edges where once there was smooth and gleaming aluminum. The water from the lake had half filled the pontoon.

Jonah frowned. "That's a problem,"

"The heck with the radio, how are we going to fix that."

For a moment Abby thought about how strapping a log to the plane would work, and she eyed some pine logs nearby, and then shook her head. They'd never get in the air with that much weight.

"I've got an idea," said Jonah as he looked around at the forest.

"Don't tell me you're thinking about strapping a log to the plane."

Jonah guffawed. "Of course not, too heavy, only a fool would consider that option."

She winced. He saw the tree he was looking for, and smiled.

"Well what then?"

He winked at her. "Old Indian trick."

"Uh oh," she began to get worried and narrowed her eyes at him. "The last time you showed me one of your old Indian tricks a bear joined the party."

"See those trees over there."

Around the bend of the cove was a stand of tall straight trees. They were mostly white with black markings where the branches used to be, the remainder of the foliage was towards the tops.

He picked up the hunting knife at the rock where he had cleaned the fish and waved his hand.

"Follow me."

"Oh brother," she sighed as she followed him. "I didn't know I was going camping with Daniel Boone."

He stood in front of the largest of the white barked trees and motioned with the palm of his hand.

"Do you know the kind of tree this is?"

She bit her lip and thought hard. 'You're a biologist for crying out loud', she told herself. "Think!" It was a strange looking tree and looked well out of place among the tall pines. It's almost as if it had gotten a foothold with one tree long ago and spread out in this one little space and made a stand of sorts against the other towering trees. She reached out and touched it and ran her hand over the surface. "It's very smooth."

"Give up?"

"Wait!" she held her hand up for a moment of silence until she knew without a doubt that her brain was totally devoid of the answer and that she was in fact after all a dunce. This was the same frustrating experience that she'd had in graduate school, you know the answer, it's stuck somewhere in there and you can't pull it up.

"Alright, alright," she finally said in exasperation. "What is it Mr. Know it all?"

He smiled with jubilation at the simplicity of the answer. "This is a Birch tree."

A wave of familiarity swept over her, of course it was a Birch tree, of course. "And this is Birch bark," she acknowledged with a sigh as she remembered her American History classes from High School.

"Yes it is. Betula papyrifera"

The Birch tree was an important tree for the Indians. The bark is flexible and waterproof, and the Indians made houses, and tepee's, fashioned water containers, music instruments, toys, sleds, shoes, and of course canoes. It was still a common tree in North America.

"So, we're going to make a birch bark canoe, like the Indians of old?"

"Not a canoe silly. We'll repair the pontoon with the bark. We'll wrap it and with a couple of sheets of bark, and tie it with…"

"Rawhide rope from a deer?"

"Funny," he said. "We have fishing line."

"Hmm, so, we're going put our trust in Birch bark on the pontoon of that plane travelling at a hundred miles an hour on the water and trust that it will still be intact when we land wherever it is we may land? Isn't that taking an old Indian trick to a new level?"

"We can also walk out," he offered. "The nearest cabin is probably around twenty miles away. Right in the direction our friend the bear headed."

"Well what are we waiting for?" she asked. "Let's get that bark off!"

He stood as tall as he could reach and cut a line straight through the bark an inch deep from the top to the bottom, and then at the top and the bottom of that line he cut a circle around the circumference of the trunk. He peeled the bark back evenly and using a stick as a straight edge, slowly rolled it off the tree.

26.

Philip Weintraub, AKA the Fox sat in the small coffee house on the outskirts of the little city of Sooke, on the southern coast of Vancouver Island, British Columbia. It was a blustery summer day, the Strait of Juan de Fuca which lay south of the island and led to the intricate waterways of the Salish Sea that intertwined through the coastal areas of western Canada was a mess of whitecaps and rain. He stayed indoors and watched the weather through the pane glass window.

The waitress was pleasant and kept his coffee filled. It was his third day in the town and his second visit to this coffee shop. It was convenient in that it had wi fi and he could keep an eye on the ocean and do his research on the laptop at the same time. He didn't like being cooped up in a room by himself, and for some strange reason he was able to think clearer out in public with a small crowd nearby. His cover story if anyone asked was that he was on holiday from England, and had always wanted to visit the sister colony. His English accent was superb and no one questioned him further. He had a single earplug for audio that he plugged into his right ear, and listened to the police scanner on the computer while he scanned the various local news outlets on the internet for a lead on the shot up plane. He flexed his hand; it was still a bit stiff, but thankfully not broken. The old farmer had put up quite a fight, and didn't go down easily. The motorcycle in the barn was a perfect vehicle for a quick cross county ride, and it sat now at the bottom of the ocean nearby after he drove it off a cliff in the middle of the night.

He cut and dyed his hair, and darkened his skin, hiked to the nearby airport before dawn and caught a taxi into town as though he'd just stepped off the early morning commuter airplane.

He checked into a small hotel on the waterfront under one of his aliases and began monitoring the news on the television and internet.

There was no word or sighting of Jonah or the bush plane. The police were all over the lab in Seattle, and the airport, they'd found the helicopter a hundred miles north of here, and the farmer. He wasn't a bit concerned, and in fact the news was inspiring since they were reporting all the details and he could sit in this little café, in a little windblown town, unnoticed and obscure, watching and waiting. Sooner or later Jonah and Abby would show up and then he would move quickly.

What he was able to glean from the reports is that the plane they were flying was a deHavilland Canada DH-2 Beaver, and it had a fully fueled range of four hundred fifty five miles. It was last produced in nineteen sixty seven and this one was outfitted with specially designed pontoons with retractable wheels. Jonah was an avid flyer and would fly into Canada and Alaska to fish on a weekly basis. The coast guard had received the report of the near collision with the fishing vessel from the captain and crew and determined that the plane matched the description of the Beaver, and the helicopter was the same one found on the north coast of Vancouver Island. They'd searched the waters in that area for three days with ships and aircraft, and had found no trace of the plane or its passengers. It was a mystery and captured the attention of half the nation for about a day, until the airways were filled with other amazing crimes and events, and the story was shuffled to the bottom of the heap.

One thing that bothered Philip was the choice of aircraft, the Beaver plane was old and slow. It was over fifty years old. With Jonah's money he could have bought the newer model DH-3 Otter with nearly double the range. There was some sort of nostalgia thing going on with that plane, and Philip had the feeling that Jonah would head for some familiar spot to regroup and gather his senses.

Jonah was on the run, that much was clear. Philip calculated that if he wanted to get to Alaska he would need to refuel along the way. Seattle to Prince Rupert at the gateway to Alaska was five hundred seventy eight miles which meant that he would need to gas up somewhere in the middle.

Posing as a reporter Philip called every airport and harbor in the area and offered a thousand dollar reward for news of a Beaver bush plane with a shot out window. No one had seen it. He left everyone his number, his untraceable cell phone that he carried as an extra. Jonah was nearby, he could sense it.

Somewhere within a hundred or so miles was a hideout in the trees, some waterway in the wilderness where he could land and stash the bush plane, somewhere he'd been before. If only there was some way get his flight log... no that was thinking way outside the box. Just wait and lay low. Tariq had sent him an encrypted message. They'd heard the news, and they wanted details. He'd sent back a three word reply, "on the trail'. They would be angry and setting up a contingency force, but what could he do. He had to stay put. His contract with the cabal was simple, make the hit and get paid, miss the hit and not only did he not get paid, he became the hit. He had never missed a target, never been caught, never tagged, so this was unchartered territory, but the rules were firm, miss the hit and get hit. There were other killers employed by the cabal. No one knew where he was and he needed to keep it that way. In a way he was as much in hiding as Jonah was. He was on the hook for the hit on Jonah and the girl, and until he got them and could prove it he needed to stay in the shadows. The cabal had a pipeline of cash set up for him that he could tap through the ATM machines, but he didn't dare go that route. There were more secretive ways to access money in a pinch.

The bell on the front door jingled and in walked two police men out of the rain, Mounties. They hung their coats and hats by the door dripping the morning rain onto the floor and walked over to the counter and sat down.

"Morning Angel," said the bigger of the two, a burly lumberjack sort of a man with a crew cut and half beard, the stool bent a little with his weight.

The other cop was shorter and skinnier with a balding head, and buggy eyes. This one scanned the diner and took note of all the customers.

The waitress stood in front of them and pulled out her pad.

"What'll it be guys? Say you look like you've been up all night."

"We have been," said the burly cop. "Someone robbed the gun store and the supermarket last night."

"What? You're joking me."

"That's right," continued the skinny cop. "They took some blasting caps from the gun shop along with the cash from the safe, then they used the caps to blast open the safe at the market."

"My Lord…"

"Over five thousand in cash," continued the burly cop.

The skinny cop lowered his voice. "And you heard about that poor old farmer Joe, up the coast."

The waitress crossed herself. "God rest his soul."

The skinny cop nodded with authority. "We've got ourselves a crime wave." He leaned over the counter and pointed surreptitiously with his thumb towards Philip in the corner. "What about that guy, what's his story?"

The waitress leaned closer to whisper back. "Oh, him? He's a real nice guy, a regular gentleman. He's on 'Oliday' from jolly old England."

The burly cop looked over at Philip and shook his head. "Naw, we're looking for a long haired blond guy, sort of pale. That guy over there has short black hair and looks like he might be part Indian." He lowered his voice. "The kind of Indian that's from India I mean."

The skinny cop scrunched his eyes and nodded. "Yeah, you're right." He pulled out a folded paper and placed it on the counter. It was a police sketch from Seattle. "You seen anyone who looks like this in the past couple of days?"

The waitress studied it, and seemed about to say something, the image did look familiar, but she shook her head. "Never saw that face in my life."

"He stole a helicopter in Seattle," continued the skinny cop. "The same one they found up north by farmer Joes. They got this picture from the security camera at the hanger."

"That guy looks creepy," said the waitress.

"Yeah," continued the skinny cop. "He killed five people in Seattle and then stole a cop car and this helicopter. They're still looking for two people, a man and woman in a bush plane."

"I saw that on the news a couple of days ago," said the waitress. "What's this world coming to?"

"You can say that again," the burly cop got up and hitched his trousers. "Well, we'd better get going. We need to stop by some of the hotels and motels in town to see if any of the people there might have seen this guy."

As they were going out the door, the skinny cop, still suspicious, walked over to Philip and asked for identification.

"Say what's this all about?" asked Philip in a thick British accent as he reached for his wallet. He pulled out a passport and handed it to the cop.

The skinny cop studied the passport. "North East Derbyshire, eh?"

"That's right."

"Never heard of it."

"East midlands, coal country."

"Are you in the coal business?"

"Accounting."

"That figures, we got a bunch of you blokes here in Vancouver too."

"Accountants?"

"Indians, from India. Funny thing is they're mostly accountants too."

"I'm not Indian sir, I'm British. My mother was Indian yes, but my father is British through and through, see my name on the passport is Willoghby, about as British a name as you'll ever find."

The skinny cop scratched his chin as he looked at the passport again.

"Yes, so there it is, Nigel Willoghby. Here on vacation are you Nigel?"

"Yes, on holiday. I've always wanted to see the Straits of Juan de Fuca. They say the winds and waves are quite spectacular."

"Yes they are," said the skinny cop. "Amazing that you should know that."

"My job is rather boring at times, so I search up the internet for interesting places to have a visit. In fact I'm planning my next trip now." He showed the cop the laptop with the map of Canada and Alaska on the screen.

The skinny cop placed the passport back on the table and tapped his forehead in a lazy salute. "Alright, sorry to bother you sir," and gathered his coat and hat and walked out the door which the burly cop held open for him.

"A regular Sherlock Holmes you are," mumbled the burly cop as he buttoned his coat and closed the door behind them.

The waitress walked over to Philip. "Another piece of pie?"

He patted his stomach. "Why yes love, I think I might have some room. Nice chaps those two."

"Oh they're just doing their job."

He beamed at her. "Say, how would you like to go to a nice restaurant tonight?"

She blushed and pushed a strand of hair back from her eyebrow. She hardly knew this guy, even though he'd sat at the café for the past two days and they'd had pleasant little conversations, about the weather and the food, and he seemed so honest, and British, she'd never dated a British man before, maybe it would be like going out with a real gentleman, like with him holding the door open for her, and pulling out the chair for her to sit in, and he had a nice smile and called her love when she had a nametag on that read Darcy, and she hesitated in all for about one second while thinking about all this and replied with her voice suddenly a little high pitched, "Okay."

27.

The pontoon was finally repaired. Jonah tightened the last knot of fishing line, and patted the bark that wrapped in layers around the metal housing.

"That ought to do it," he said.

Abby stood on the bank and clapped. "Good job."

"Now to test it out," said Jonah, and he pushed the plane out onto the lake until he was standing in waist deep water. He took out his flashlight and peered into the access hole on top of the pontoon. He had already drained the water out with a hand pump and hose and although the interior was still damp with moisture, no new water was entering. He bounced the pontoon up and down on the water and waited a few minutes before proclaiming success and screwed the plug back into the hole, and then gently landed the aircraft on the bank and retied the anchor line.

Abby was back at work on the radio which she had removed from the plane and taken it completely apart, it lay in pieces on a towel on the ground. A bullet had gone straight through it buckling the case and severing wires. She was able to splice the wires back together but there was a bigger hurdle to cross.

"What do you think?" asked Jonah.

"I wish I had a soldering gun."

The bullet had grazed the motherboard and some wires were separated from it. The silver dabs of solder that held the wires to the board were intact, but without the wires attached it was worthless.

"How about super glue?" And as soon as he said it realized his folly. "Never mind," he said and corrected himself. "Super glue does not conduct electricity."

She laughed. "Of course it doesn't. Got any old Indian tricks?"

"We could send out smoke signals."

"Funny. So now what?"

"We wait," said Jonah. "We're safe here, well as long as we don't get any more big furry moochers."

"That's not a happy thought."

"We have food and water and shelter. The weather is calm. Let's wait a couple of more days, and head back down. Hopefully by then everything's been settled, and they found the assassin. If not, we stay in hiding."

"How will we find out if they caught him?"

"We need a radio or cell phone. There's a small harbor near here out on the coast. I've used it before. We'll fly in, refuel, grab some supplies and a marine radio and get back in the air, it'll take about half an hour. Let's give it two more days and head to the coast."

"It's fine with me; I could actually stay here a

lot longer than a couple of days." She breathed deep. "I've never smelled air this fresh."

He smiled. "Yeah this is God's country alright."

She shrugged. "Maybe."

"You really don't believe in God do you?"

"I believe in what can I see and hear and smell and touch.""Can you see the moon that's over the horizon and getting ready to rise in a couple of hours?"

"No, but I have seen it, as a matter of fact I saw it yesterday when it rose, and I know from data that it will rise an hour later today and the next day another hour later. I can see where this is going, and I don't want to get into an argument on whether or not there is an all knowing all seeing God sitting in a place called heaven like Michelangelo's Sistine Chapel painting."

"We don't have to argue, we can at least talk about it, like adults."

She narrowed her eyes at him.

"Like adult scientists," he continued.

"Okay, I do believe in a type of God, just not some old wise man with a long beard sitting on top of a hill."

"Well, I don't know about that either, but there's one I do know with all the certainty in the world, we didn't make ourselves." He picked up a pebble by his shoe and held it up. "We couldn't even make this little rock. Sure we could rearrange some elements, gather up some material and squish it together but we can't make the elements themselves. Well, except for me that is, I can make gas."

She laughed and threw a pebble at him. "You're gross!"

"Sorry, that one just slipped out. Remember, we're having a discussion." He ducked and shielded his face as she threw another pebble at him.

"Like adult scientists, hello?" She admonished him while tossing the projectile.

He held his hand up in a peace symbol. "Sorry I got that one from my Dad, he used that line in a similar situation. These are kind of discussions we used to have when I was in my 'Super Scientist' phase when I was in my late teens, thought I knew it all, and actively rebelling against anything and everything, including the thought of an all seeing omnipotent being other than myself."

"I'm not being selfish," she said. "I just think it's kind of silly, and a waste of time for people to sit around praying to someone who they've never seen, and only been told about by someone who had it told to them, and that other person had it told to them, and so on and so on, like a giant ponzi scheme, and on top of that if you don't believe, then you get sent to some lake of fire for all eternity. Whatever happened to free will?"

"Okay, I think you might have something about that one. Maybe it's kind of like 'yes you do have free will', but you're wasting time by not at least acknowledging a higher power, since getting back to the original argument, no jokes this time, we cannot make the basic elements from scratch, and being a scientist you have to admit that since nothing just appears out of thin air so to speak, they must have been created by a higher power. And if there is a higher power that is so powerful it can make something so incredible, this universe, this little pebble, us, then maybe we should tip our hat a little once in a while, give some credit where credit is due, and sometimes, not all the time of course, but sometimes just try to use our cognizant powers, and connect with that higher power and be polite, and say thank you. Isaac Newton said 'Gravity explains how the planets are in motion, but it doesn't explain who set them in motion in the first place."

They lit the Dakota fire pit and cooked the fish they'd caught that afternoon, Trout and Pike and Walleye. Abby kept a keen eye out for anything big and furry, she had calmed down over the course of the past two days since the bear had rambled through the camp, and now she had the habit of glancing at the woods nearby every few minutes without even noticing she was doing it, and in the back of her thoughts she knew exactly how far it was to the tree that she climbed.

"You never told me why your wife left you."

"Hasn't crossed my mind in a long time. I'd almost forgotten about it, thanks."

"Sorry, but there's no television up here to watch, and since we're being so 'open' in our conversation…"

"Yeah, we'll it wasn't very complicated at all." He shrugged his shoulders. "I like to go camping, a lot, and she found out after a while that she didn't."

Abby tried to hold back her giggles.

"What?"

"Nothing, it's just that I've been on one of your camping trips."

"Hey, they're not always this fun. Sometimes they're downright boring."

"Did she ever remarry?"

"Yeah, a real steady guy too. Banker, a regular stick in the mud, never leaves the city, never gets his hands dirty, a real peach of a guy, Eddie Bartkowski, steady Eddie and his wife Lucy. She met him while I was on one of my camping trips without her. Go figure."

He tossed a small log into fire pit.

"And you?"

"Oh I'm actually happy for her, she was miserable with me. Plus I'm happy for me that she found someone so quick. No alimony." He winked at her. "But I'm available if that's what you mean."

"I mean do you ever think you might take the plunge again?"

"Oh I don't know, she'd have to like going camping, that's for sure."

They finished their meal of fish and corn and rehydrated potatoes and sat back to watch the sun's rays filter through the trees in the late afternoon when suddenly a high pitched whistle shot through the air and Abby jumped to her feet ready to run to her tree. On the opposite bank of the lake stood a man whistling with all his might and waving his hands. He whistled again three times and kept waving.

"Someone's in trouble," said Jonah.

Her voice edged with fear. "What's going on?"

He pulled the binoculars from the pack nearby and trained them on the whistler. "It's the universal hunters distress call, either three shots in the air, or three whistles, it means the same, somebody needs help."

"How do you know it's not some sort of trick, maybe the assassin found us."

"If they found us we'd know it. We'd be hearing bullets whistling over our heads, not Cree Johnson whistling."

"Cree Johnson, what are you talking about?"

"I know that guy." Jonah waved with his free hand, and the whistler waved for them to come to the other shore. "He's a local. An Indian guide from the coast, I see two hunters with him dressed in camouflage with orange caps. One of them is lying on the ground, might be hurt."

Jonah put the binoculars down and started for the plane, "Let's go. Grab the first aid kit in the back."

With Abby in the plane he pushed it hard from the shore and walked along the pontoon to the cockpit. "It's too far to paddle," he explained as he sat in the pilot's seat and turned the ignition.

The engine chugged to life and he gave the throttle a nudge and the plane started across the short stretch of water. When he was about a hundred yards from shore he cut the engine, grabbed the paddle and went onto the back of the pontoon and guided the plane to the shore like a canoe. Cree Johnson stood waist deep in the water and caught the leading edge of the pontoon slowing the craft and bringing it onshore.

Cree Johnson looked like he stepped out of a book on American Indians. His hardened face with a dark reddish complexion, the distinguished nose long and flattened at the end set on a face that was chiseled out of the skin of a catcher's mitt, tough and lined. His black hair was short and wild on top, with two long pony tails on the sides. His eyes both dark and terrible and kind at the same time, with a calm solemn demeanor barely containing an underlying warrior ferocity.

He reached out to help Abby to the shore, his hand felt rough and hard like the bark of an ancient tree, or the asphalt on a well travelled road, and as she touched his shoulder and swung herself to the beach she thought to herself that the shoulder must be part granite and bone.

"Sure glad to see you Jonah," said Cree.

"Someone hurt?"

"Not much, just a bit. Come look."

Jonah tied the plane to a big rock and motioned Abby to follow.

"This is George and Harold," said Cree as he pointed to the two hunters. Harold was lying on a makeshift litter made from pine branches. His foot was bundled in a swath of cloth tinged with red and he did not look happy.

"When?"

"This morning about nine."

Jonah motioned for Abby to take a look.

"This is Abby, she's a doctor."

Abby knelt down next to Harold and took his wrist and felt for his pulse with one hand and placed her other on his forehead. "How are you doing?" She smiled at him with a mixture of concern, and strength.

"It's pretty sore ma'am."

"No fever, pulse is steady, let's have a look okay?"

He nodded and she scooted down to the bundle of bloody rags and slowly untied the mess.

"Single shot, small bullet, twenty two caliber, went straight through," said Cree.

"Shot yourself in the damn foot!" exclaimed George.

"Will you let it go?" pleaded Harold. "Can't you see I'm in pain?" He propped himself up on an elbow so he could see what Abby was doing.

"What was your plan," Jonah asked Cree. "Gonna hike him all the way out of here?"

"Yeah well, they wanted to go in old style, no communication with the outside world. Made me leave my cell phone and radio at the lodge. Normally I'd just call for help and it'd be here in an hour."

"Hear that Harold? Had to go in old style like

an old Indian warrior, and then shot yourself in the foot." George was obviously enjoying this. Harold just shook his head and said nothing, then finally.

"Will you give it a rest?"

Abby shot an icy glance at George and he winced. "Alright, I was just funnin'."

"It's okay," said Harold. "I'm a klutz."

The bandage was off and Abby was wiping the wound with gauze. It was a perfectly round hole that went straight through the top of the foot to the bottom.

"Good thing it was a small caliber," she said and was matter of fact with her assessment.

"The bleeding has stopped. You probably have some cartilage and ligament damage, it looks like it went right in between two of the metatarsals bones, but we can't be sure without an x-ray. You'll be on crutches for a while, but nothing that can't be fixed." She tossed the old rag on the side and bandaged the foot with new gauze and taped it, then wrapped it with elastic.

"It's going to be dark in about half an hour," said Jonah. He looked at his watch, it was half past ten. This far north in midsummer meant nearly twenty hours of daylight.

"We'll camp for the night and take off around four this morning when it's light. I can fly at night, but I don't want to risk it, too many mountains in the way. Think you can hold on for another couple of hours?"

Harold nodded, wincing in pain as Abby

finished wrapping his foot. "I'm okay."

"Have you taken any pain medication?" she asked him.

Harold shook his head.

"Look in the side pouch of the medicine bag Abby," said Jonah. 'There's a couple of Percocet's and a flask of brandy. That should fix him up." Jonah winked at Abby as Harold drank the brandy. "For medicinal purposes."

They helped Harold into the plane and settled him into the back seat. He was feeling the effects of the medication and was singing softly. "Over the hills and through the woods to Grand mama's house we go…"

Cree was inspecting the bark wrapped around the front of the pontoon. "Nice work, got a leak?"

"Little one," said Jonah. "I'll tell you about it later."

Abby and the other passengers crowded into the plane and Jonah pushed off from the bank. Within a few minutes they were back on the island.

"You're missing the back window," said George.

"Yeah, a tree branch fell on it," Jonah lied.

"Are we there yet?" mumbled Harold and then he fell fast asleep.

They left Harold snoring in the plane and sat around the Dakota Fire pit. Jonah filled the hole with dry wood and lit it. "It's safer over here on the island," he said, and then checked himself.

"Mostly."

"The wolves," Cree nodded. "Every year there are more and more."

"We'll build a big fire," said Jonah "and take turns keeping watch. I'm not worried about wolves so much as bears. We had big one pay us a visit a couple of days ago."

"How big?" asked Cree.

"Really big," said Jonah "weighed over a grand."

Cree whistled. "Male?"

"I didn't get close enough to find out"

"Missing a front toe?"

"Again Cree, I didn't count 'em."

"Hunches to the right, like this." Cree did his best bear imitation.

"You know, it actually did."

"Streak of white by his cheek?"

Jonah squinted, thinking hard, picturing it in his mind when he was taking aim over the bears head. "Yeah, there was a streak of white."

"That's Big Ben!" Cree slapped his thigh, genuinely happy at solving the puzzle.

"You name the bears up here?" asked Abby.

"Well, just that one. Every once in a while he makes it down to the town, scares the crap, oops sorry ma'am, scares the heck out of everyone. It's against the law to shoot a Grizzly, so they call the game warden, he calls animal control, and they chase Big Ben around the town for awhile, tranquilize him and fly him way back up into the mountains again. It's been a couple of years since we've seen him."

"You can add a physical characteristic to your list," said Jonah.

"What's that?"

"He's missing part of an ear now." Jonah pointed his index finger like a gun.

"You shot him?"

"Well, shot at him is more the case. I was trying to scare him off and he moved at the last second."

"Good thing the feds didn't see it."

"You're not a fed are you?" Jonah asked George.

"Naw, I'm a car salesman." he handed Jonah a business card from his top pocket.

"Landmark Auto, Seattle."

Jonah frowned. "What, even out here?"

"Old habit, but hey you never know, everyone needs a car, right?"

"A plane comes in more handy around here pal." They all laughed at that.

George was looking at Abby. "Say Miss?"

"It's Abby," she said.

"Abby, I wanted to apologize for being kind of rude back there to Harold."

"He was in a lot of pain."

"I know, I was just trying to keep him upbeat, that's how we keep each other sharp. We rib each other a lot, all day long actually, it helps us stay focused. You see, we're in a tough business, and no one really wants to come in and talk to us. Sure they have to when they need a new car, but they don't really want to. The rankings go like this, from least to most desirable: Car salesman, Dentist, IRS attorney, Grim Reaper. You get the picture, we have no illusions."

"Yeah, you guys really do have a bad reputation."

"I love that guy like a brother."

"He'll be okay."

"You gotta admit though, it's pretty stupid to shoot yourself in the foot." George laughed. "Man, I'm gonna get a lot mileage out of this one!"

"How long have you been out?" Jonah asked Cree.

"Five days. We were scheduled to start heading down tomorrow. They bagged two trophies, but we had to leave the antlers after the accident, too much to carry."

"Shot himself in the foot huh?"

"Yeah it was the darn'dest thing. Harold had just brought down a big bull moose from about three hundred yards out, we were hiding in the forest and the bull was in a clearing. The moose falls to the ground and out from the other side comes a pack of wolves and just tears into the moose. They must have been tracking him also, just on the other side of the clearing. Harold got so excited he tried to shoot at the pack to get them away from his trophy, but his rifle jammed, so he reached for his pistol on his hip, he was wearing it like he was a gunfighter from the old west or something. Anyways he grabs for his pistol, and I'm telling him not to bother as it was no use, and he must have pulled the trigger before he got the gun out of the holster. He turned white as a ghost and fell right to the ground; the shock of what he done just knocked the wind right out of him."

George started to say something and Abby frowned at him.

"Well," he started and after noticing Abby's piercing gaze he turned serious, "that was not a fun part of the day. We thought he'd shot himself in the heart or something worse, thought he was dead. Then he started howling and we found out it was it was his foot he shot. He was howling so loud he almost succeeded in chasing away the wolves; they thought a rival wolf pack had them surrounded, and they started howling back." He looked sheepishly at Abby before continuing and decided not to laugh. "That's a sight you don't see every day."

Cree did chuckle though. "That is definitely a sight you don't see every day. I mean you can get wolves to howl easy enough, I've done it plenty of times, just give 'em a howl and they'll howl right back sure enough, but these wolves were going off I tell ya, I think his howl of pain really got to 'em."

They built a good sized campfire to the side and Jonah used the Dakota fir pit to cook up the remaining fish.

"So how do you two know each other?" Abby asked Cree.

"Him?" Cree motioned at Jonah with

puzzlement on his face. "I don't know him."

Abby was confused, her face contorted in disbelief. "But," she stammered, "Jonah knew your name, he said so when he saw you with his binoculars, and you said glad to see you Jonah when we got to the other side of the lake, I'm sure I heard that."

Cree and Jonah both laughed. "I'm just kidding you Abby," said Cree. "I've known this honcho since we were little squirts, we've gotten into more trouble when we were kids than the days are long."

"My Dad and Cree's dad were old friends," Jonah explained. "They went to college together, played on the baseball team, and when they graduated they kept in touch and when I was about ten or so we'd come up here and go on extended camping trips. Cree and I are the same age."

"Born a day apart," said Cree. "I'm older so I get to tell him what to do."

"Yeah right," Jonah smirked. "I'll put you in a headlock if your want."

Cree rubbed his neck just thinking about it, he had a pinched nerve from carrying the liter with Harold in it down the mountain. "I think I better pass on that. Too old today, talk to me tomorrow."

Abby was suspicious. "So you used to get in a lot of trouble huh?"

"Holy cow," Cree shook his head, suddenly jolted to the past. "Remember Barton, Jonah?"

Jonah winced. "Oh yeah…"

"So it was like this Abby," said Cree. "Me and this other kid didn't like each other for nothin' growing up. He was ornery and I was ornery, and maybe it's the same way with girls, I don't know, but you get to 'not' liking someone and there is nothing that can be done about it, you're enemies through and through, and it was like that with me and Barton O'Conner. His parents were rich and owned the dock and half the town. My parents were sort of poor and scraping along. That was strike number one. Strike number two was he was a good baseball player and he got to play short stop, pitcher, third base, all the good spots, and I was kind of clumsy and relegated to the outfield, right field where hardly any one hit the ball. He'd really rub that in on me, always winking at me as I made my way to the outfield, with a shit eating grin on his face. Strike three was him hitting on Sally Winifield, the prettiest girl in a hundred miles, hair like golden silk, face like an angel."

Abby was smiling, this was a great story. For some reason girls always enjoyed the thought of more than one boy fighting over her, it was some sort of a primal thing that went back to the caveman days.

"So here we are," continued Cree. "Two kids, ten years old and mortal enemies, but me, I'm an Indian you see, so there's a bit of savage blood cooking in my veins, even from a young age. I was clumsy, but cunning. Then along comes poor

Jonah, smart as a whip and tough in his own right and ready for action, and now I have a sidekick, kind of like the Green Hornet and Tonto. And I dragged him into my scheme."

Jonah sighed. "Oh Brother,"

Cree went on. "So we start cooking up schemes to torture old Barton, and so one day we laid in wait for him on his way home from baseball practice, threw a sack over him and tied him to a red ant hill for a while, just like the old Indians used to do to their enemies. The ants were crawling all over him, under his clothes, in his ears, through his hair. He was screaming bloody murder, it was echoing through the whole forest, and some fishermen heard him wallowing and came by and let him go. Old Barton swelled up like a balloon from all the bites, had to go to the hospital for a couple of days. He never saw us, no one could pin it on us, but our parents had their suspicions. And then we had our best attack idea of the century. There was a big bee hive in the nook of an old oak tree near the library. Everyone knew it was there and the beekeeper was going to take it away the next day so we had to work fast. During the night we got a ladder and fishing line and while the bees were sleeping we tied a loop around the hive and hid the line down the trunk of the tree…"

"I don't like where this is going," said Abby.

"… and then we got a soccer ball and smothered it with raw honey…"

George was leaning forward with a smile on

his face, he loved pranks.

"...we hid by the tree and when we saw old Barton walking by I yelled out to him, 'Hey Barton, you think you're such a great baseball player, let's see you try to catch this!', and then I threw the ball high in the air, and the big dummy dropped the books he was carrying and got all serious and caught it. I could never forget, his face had a look of triumph, and then he noticed all that his hands were sticky from the honey. Jonah yanked the fishing line, the bee hive came tumbling out of the tree and that pack of bees being naturally pissed off from being suddenly homeless, and swarming for revenge, smelled the honey on Barton's hands and took off after him like a swirling cloud of stingers. He ran like a banshee down the road with a thousand bees on his tail. We fell on the ground laughing, I'll tell you we couldn't breathe we were laughing so hard."

"It was pretty funny, for a while," Jonah admitted.

"Yeah, and then we looked over and saw that the librarian was standing at the doorway with her hands on her hips. She had seen the whole thing, and went inside and called our parents. You couldn't get away with anything in that dang town."

"Let me guess, hospital?"

"Turns out 'ol Barton was allergic to bees, damn near killed him."

"Our Dad's beat the tar out of us, but they

had no choice." Jonah winced again and then chuckled. "Good times."

"So did your plan work?" asked Abby.

"What plan?"

"You know, pummel the rival, get the girl."

Cree shook his head. "Naw, I drove her into his arms, she felt sorry for him and ran to the hospital, said I was a jerk and they've been together ever since."

"So did they live happily ever after like a fairy tale romance?"

Cree smiled a crooked smile. "That's the best part. Old Barton's henpecked, Sally's rounder than a beach ball, and in her words her 'good for nothing husband will never be able to make enough money to keep her happy'. She's like a vacuum cleaner at an all you can eat buffet."

" 'Ol Cree dodged a bullet."

"You can say that again."

"Did you ever marry."

"Of course! I'm a full blooded Indian. We marry and have plenty papoose, make the tribe strong." He made a fist and growled. "Around the same time there was this girl, no one really took much notice of her, she was lanky and goofy, and not too good looking when we were ten. Braces, glasses, shy, the works, but I'll tell you right about when she turned sixteen, look out! It was like one summer she was as plain a rock…"

Abby was laughing in shock.

"…I'm telling you true, plain as a dull rock in a field full of flowers, and the next thing you know she bloomed into the prettiest flower in that field. Just kablaam!, out of nowhere. It seemed like one day she would walk by and no one would even notice, it would be like, 'did someone feel a breeze? Did a cloud go by the sun? Something insignificant has happened to make us pause.' And then we'd keep talking, as though in fact nothing had happened of much significance, or meaning. And the next day she walked by and all conversation halted, everyone's mouth open in awe, a guy would forget his own name. It was crazy, out of nowhere. And you know she's kept that beauty, it has stuck to her like the air is stuck to the earth, mystical and benevolent and kind."

"Your wife?" asked Abby.

"Fifteen years, eight kids, my Rose Marie, half Cree, half Chicano, best cook and wife in the whole northwest. It's funny how life works out."

"That's an amazing story."

"I like the part about the bees," said George as he leaned against a log.

Abby frowned at him.

"And Jonah is a confirmed bachelor, as far as we know." Cree winked at Abby and her cheeks reddened.

When they'd had their fill, they threw the remains far out into the lake and laid down next to the fire.

"I'll take the full watch," Cree said to Jonah. "You need your rest so you can fly us out safe at daylight."

Jonah started to protest and then realizing the

wisdom of it as well as the fact that he was never going to win an argument against it, he got some blankets from the plane for himself and Abby. Harold was still snoring and he closed the doors securely. Cree wrapped himself in his Indian blanket with his back to a tree, and with his rifle at his side settled in to watch over the camp.

The quiet sound of the forest nestled around them, and as the three slowly fell to sleep, from far off in the distant mountains, the lonely howl of a wolf wafted over the water like a lullaby.

Stars circled overhead in the moonless night for a short while and then a hint of dawn formed towards the east, casting a halo on the distant mountain peaks.

The morning crept over them, grey and cold, while a silent mist formed on the lake that was still as ice.

Cree stood by the water's edge watching across the lake as a mother deer and her doe drank on the other side. A big buck stood guard nearby, and a bald Eagle floated on the airways searching for prey in the water below. This was his favorite time of the day, and of the year, the summertime when the days were long and full of plenty. The dawn would come slowly enough, creeping through the woods, silent and steady, first grey and then gold and then the bright and shining summer sun lasting for twenty hours or more, but by the time the gold hit the water today they would be back down the mountain, and he would be looking for another tour to take into the wilderness. It was a great life in the north in the summer. The winter though was hard and bleak, and he needed to work to make it through the long cold and rainy, and dark days and nights ahead, and care for his family. The buck on the other side looked at Cree and their eyes met.

"We are much alike, you and I," thought Cree. "Standing watch."

Without a sound the mother deer and doe walked past the buck and into the forest disappearing from sight. The buck watched Cree until they were well into the trees and then turned and followed.

Cree heard a stone rustle behind him and knew it was Jonah walking towards him. They stood side by side for a while watching the other side of the lake, silent.

"That was a nice sized buck," said Jonah.

"Ten pointer, not bad."

"What's the biggest you've seen lately?"

"Twelve pointer late last year, the other side of the mountain, right before the snows came. I was with a tour, we tried to get close for a shot, but he was too smart for us, or the folks in the tour were too loud, probably both. What about you, been fishing much?"

"No, this is the first time in about a month."

"Been busy being a scientist?"

"Yup."

"So what kind of trouble are you in?"

Jonah looked at Cree.

"No trouble."

"Don't try to be secret with me Jonah. I didn't want to say anything with the others around, but I know you're in danger. I saw the bullet holes in the plane cab, the back window blown out, and don't try to tell me a tree branch did that, the radio." He hesitated before continuing, "…the girl."

"It's complicated."

"I'm your brother. Your blood brother since we were small, you became part of our tribe when we were kids Jonah. That ceremony wasn't just for show, that bond cannot be broken. We're supposed to help each other no matter what. The Great Spirit caused you to fly here, and also for Harold to shoot himself in the foot so we would need to come down the mountain and find you. Events like this don't happen on their own. Even you can agree with that. Scientific data be damned."

"Yeah, well." Jonah looked back at the campfire, and Abby sleeping peacefully.

They were in danger, he'd almost forgotten how much, being up here in the wilderness, enveloped in the security of the woods, fishing, breathing in the clean open spaces. Even the contact with the bear seemed completely natural, a part of the sphere of creation that existed without which any scientific data was useless rock counting, and he'd relished being here, but that time was soon coming to an end.

"Whatever it is you can stay with us. We have men and guns, places to hide. No one is going to mess with us, you know that."

Jonah shook his head. "There are some people after us, I don't know how many or who they are. Professional killers. I don't want anyone else to get involved."

"How in the heck does a scientist get in such trouble? Is it the girl; is she someone else's woman?"

"No, Abby's a scientist. We've been working together on a project. We discovered something, made it actually, and now some very bad people want to get their hands on it, and us."

"I see, they want to steal from you." He spit on the ground before continuing, a thief was worse than vile spit on a rock and he reminded himself of this fact with this gesture. "Greed and envy, it is the bane of humanity. It destroys the spirit, imprisons the heart and poisons and rots the mind, it shackles a man to the demons and condemns him to damnation in the place we do not speak of. As the good book says 'a man should not covet his neighbor's possessions', and the fools do not listen." He spit again. "And you can't go to the authorities?" He suddenly felt stupid asking that. A man should be able to defend himself from a thief without going to any authority other than God himself.

"I don't know who to trust yet."

"And so you come to the wilderness, where you can be on more equal footing, is this your plan? To bring the fight to familiar territory, where you can have an advantage?"

"Right now I'm just trying to hide out until I find out more about who's after us."

"I am telling you Jonah we can hide you. There are places even you do not know of in these woods, where no airplane can reach."

"Not a chance. These people are worse than you can imagine, they have spies everywhere. They had a camera the size of a housefly in my lab. I need to fly you all back down the mountain, and then get as far away as possible. People will see us when we land and take back off, but they cannot see you. We'll need to find a way to hide you, pull up next to a shed by the side of the airfield if possible."

They flew through the mountain passes towards the ocean in the distance. Behind them the orange glow of the sunrise illuminated the towering peaks, while far ahead was the glint of a water filled horizon and a hint of blue ocean. Cree was sitting in the co-pilots seat and was intent on searching the land below. There were many places in the valleys that he would like to visit with a hunting party, cracks and crevices in the walls of the passes that harbored game.

"Remember that spot we used to go to with your Dad?" asked Cree. "The hole in the wall, next to the Old Man?"

Jonah sighed a little as he remembered, and smiled. The Old Man was a peculiar mountain peak twenty miles from the coast, round and treeless, like a huge bald head. "He found it on an aerial map. Impossible to get to by plane or even helicopter, no place to land, overhangs, cross winds, downdrafts, but a little Shangri la for hunting and fishing, we finally had to hike in. That was a fun time, you ever been back?"

"Naw, too hard to get to. It's just over that ridge, what do you say we take a spin over it on our way down?"

Jonah glanced back at his passengers. "This isn't the time for a sightseeing tour." Thinking of his Dad though made him reconsider, and he nodded at Cree. "Well, it is on the way, sort of. How are you guys doing back there?" he practically had to yell over the wind coming through the open back window.

Abby was huddled against the side behind Jonah with her head wrapped in a blanket to keep her hair from flying all over the cabin.

"What?" she shouted.

"I said how are you doing?" he yelled again.

"Oh just peachy!" she shouted back.

Harold was laying motionless on the middle row of seats strapped in and sleeping while George was sitting next to Abby in one of the back two jump seats. His face was pale and he nodded feebly towards Jonah. He was clutching a brown paper bag between his legs but he hadn't needed to use it yet. "I get a little airsick," he told Abby for the fifth time.

"Just keep looking at the horizon out the window," she replied to him gently, also for the fifth time. "Your brain and inner ear need to have a point of reference with all the bouncing going on."

Jonah banked the plane to the left and rose up and over a wooded ridge. The weighted feeling of going up and then the weightless feeling of going down nearly sent George over the edge and he gulped and kept his eyes on the horizon. Straight ahead was a mountain shaped like a dome, round on top with straight edges on the side, mostly granite, pile driven out of the subterranean earth by continent sized plates grinding against each other over the past five million years. Very few trees were able to gain a foothold on the hardened surface, and in the summer months it stood out like a sore thumb among the tree shrouded mountains and valleys that surrounded it.

They flew straight towards it and then glided along the northern wall and a large and rugged valley that had formed next to the mountain, it towered above them on the left and Abby had a great view and she leaned her face against the window looking up at the cliff face leading to the round top. A wide stream flowed along the valley at the base of the old man, and they followed it as it wound its way around the mountain. The stream frothed in places with rapids, and gentle calm areas, and then as they neared the middle of the width of the mountain a waterfall plummeted a thousand feet to a short hanging valley where the stream was calm and protected on two sides by the steep walls of the mountain and the valley that had been slowly eroded over the eons by the waterfall. They circled once over the hanging valley, marveling at its construction and then there was another big waterfall and a series of smaller waterfalls as the stream and valley left the shadow of the Old Man, and continued on its way along the now gently sloping terrain towards the sea.

"Best fishing I've ever seen," said Jonah. "I don't know how the fish got there with those giant waterfalls guarding the entrance to the sea, but they are there."

Abby was still looking back at the mountain and the two waterfalls framing the northern side of the Old Man, and suddenly the view of the two waterfalls jogged her memory. There was a picture on the wall of Jonah's office, a big round and bald mountain with two giant waterfalls next to it, with Jonah as a kid holding a trout next to his Dad, a cherished photo of a time gone by, and this was the place. As they flew forward, Abby kept looking back at the mountain fading in the distance, while bits of bark floated in their wake. She pressed her face against the glass and down at the pontoon as the last bit of birch bark parted from the float and blew into the wind.

The gaping hole at the front of the pontoon, normally aerodynamically smooth grabbed the wind and the sudden drag slowed the airspeed and pulled the plane to the left.

Jonah shouted as he struggled to keep control. "The pontoon!" yelled Abby from the back, and Jonah looked out the window and seeing the gaping hole notched back on the throttle to further slow the plane down and it steadied itself and flew straight.

"Can you still land?" asked Cree.

Jonah scrunched his face. "A sea landing is out of the question, that pontoon will fill with water on impact and sink and we'll flip the plane. We don't have enough gas to get to an airport, so we'll have to find an empty road and use the wheels."

Jonah looked at Cree. "I need another pontoon to get to my next destination. There won't be any roads where I'm going."

Cree nodded. "There's a DH-2 Beaver at the harbor. Last I saw it was under repair in a hanger by the wharf. We can land at the service road and taxi to the hanger and switch pontoons. It's four AM on a Sunday morning so the service road should be clear of traffic. The hanger is locked but there's a key in the Harbor Masters office on the dock."

Jonah scanned the horizon. The sky was empty and clear, not a cloud in sight, the pink and blue midsummer dawn was spreading towards the west and the sleepy coastal village. He brought the plane down to two hundred feet and engaged the flaps and the little bush plane slowed to a crawl as he lined up the service highway that paralleled the coast and led to the small boat harbor.

The service road led from the harbor to the old cannery that was beaten and broken down now, a rusted twist of metal near the railway leading out of town. The decline of the salmon stock nearby and competition from the big companies up north put it out of business twenty years in the past. The service road was only about four hundred yards long and it looked like it hadn't been used in four hundred years. Jonah grimaced. "That's our only option?"

"It's the longest road in town," said Cree. "How much room do you need?"

"About half that, if I'm good," said Jonah as they flew slowly over the road and circled once over it. It was pockmarked and there were a couple of abandoned cars scattered along the edges, and one large rusted truck at the front entrance to the cannery. Jonah noted one section that looked better than the rest, it was right in front of the cannery by the truck, and he pointed to it as they cruised over it. "That's our target."

Jonah kept going straight, a mile away from the cannery, and then banked into a long slow turn and headed back towards the road. He lined the nose of the plane directly onto the roof of the cannery and turned in his seat to shout instructions.

"Alright everybody, strap in and get ready to land, and hang onto your hats." He looked towards the back to make sure everyone had heard and when he saw the wide eyes of his passengers it was quite evident that they had heard the command.

He brought the airspeed down to seventy five miles an hour, stall speed for the Beaver was sixty miles an hour and he needed to ride close to that number to make the short landing. He came in low over the cannery, they could see down into the interior of the building as it swept by, holes in the roof, rusted metal beams, and then they were over the entrance and the rusted truck. He pushed the joystick down and the nose of the plane angled towards the road the airspeed increased with the slight dive, and just as disaster and the pocked road was about to hit them he pulled back on the stick and cut the engine.

The plane nearly stalled and then leveled out and bounced loud and hard on the asphalt at sixty miles an hour. Jonah quickly engaged the reverse thrust for the propeller, and they lurched to the left and then the right as the wheels screeched and smoked and grabbed for traction and then some smaller bumps and they coasted to a stop.

"Hey that wasn't so bad," Jonah nodded to Cree and looked back at his petrified passengers in the back seats. George had his head between his knees, and Harold was still half asleep lifting his head groggily from the seat, and had no idea what had just happened. Abby crossed herself with her eyes closed and let out a gentle sigh.

"Pull up to the harbor base yard straight ahead," said Cree. "There's a small hanger on the side with the bush plane inside. I'll go to the harbor master's house and get the key."

The plane bumped slowly along the old beaten road, some of the potholes were deeper than the wheels were high and the pontoons scraped on the asphalt in those places and Jonah grimaced at the grating sound. In time they taxied up to a fenced base yard filled with old boats and trailers.

Even though it was four in the morning there were fishermen working on vessels here and there and getting them ready for the sea, coiling rope, loading rods and tackle, filling ice containers, and some just standing around talking. They all stopped what they were doing and watched the bush plane approaching, and then went back to their business at hand.

Standing next to the fence was an old metal airplane hangar; its large sliding doors were shut with a large padlock on the front. Jonah turned off the engine as they got closer and used the brake as the suddenly silent plane glided to a stop in front of the hanger.

The harbor masters house was a brick and stone office set at the edge of the water in the middle of the small harbor. Its main windows faced out towards the ocean and the entrance to the bay and it had in times past been used to monitor traffic in and out of the once prosperous port. Now it was an old and faded relic in need of paint and plaster where the remaining tenants of the harbor paid their rent for use of the storage and boat ramp.

"I'll use the phone in the office to call my Dad, and he can take George and Harold to the doctor in town," said Cree as he exited the plane.

28.

The black cell phone buzzed on the table next to the bed. Philip Weintraub lifted his head off the pillow and reached for it.

"Hello?"

"John Mack?"

The fake name he was using as his reporter alias. "Speaking."

"This is Barton O'Conner up at Johnson Harbor sir. You called the other day about the bush plane?"

He sat up quickly and slid out of bed. "Yes, yes Barton, any news?"

"Well yes sir, a plane landed this morning, just a few minutes ago actually and it matches the description, a White deHavilland Beaver DH-2, no back window."

Philip went to the window and looked out at the grey and windswept Strait of Juan de Fuca. "Are they still there?" he asked.

Barton was looking out the harbor masters window with binoculars, the shades drawn to hide him. He could see his old nemesis Jonah Mclean in the pilot's seat and that ever present thorn in his side the half breed Cree Johnson climbing out of the plane. His blood boiled whenever he caught sight of that Indian. It was a strange coincidence that he came to the harbor office so early in the morning, and what a stroke of luck if he could somehow cause some trouble for those two and make a coin or two on top of it.

"Yes sir," continued Barton. "It looks like there's something wrong with one of the landing gear, the pontoon, I can see it from where I'm standing, and it looks smashed."

Philip clenched his fist. "Bit of a problem eh?"

"Well, they barely made the landing on an old road nearby. I don't think they can take off in the condition it's in now. I see Jonah MacLean in the pilot's seat and there is a young woman in one of the rear seats."

The knuckles of Philip's fist turned white as he spoke. "Excellent work Barton, absolutely outstanding. Now then, there's the small matter of a reward."

Phillip could hear the sigh of relief on the other end of the phone. "Why yes sir, I was hoping you'd remember about that."

"Of course, of course a deal is a deal. Now you just give me your full name and address and I'll have my secretary at the newspaper write up a check and mail it to you right away."

As Barton relayed his contact info Philip wrote in the air with his pinkie, dotting I's and crossing tees. "Got it, now you have a nice day Barton, and thanks again," as he clicked the phone's off button.

His waitress friend Darcy was rubbing sleepy

eyes with her head on the pillow. "Who was that love?"

One night together and she was already prying into his business. He was pleasant and smiled at her. "Oh just work love, now you go back to sleep, I'll be going out for a cup of coffee in a moment and bring some back for the both of us." He patted her gently on the head and she smiled and nuzzled back under the covers with a sigh.

He flipped open his laptop and logged onto the internet and searched up a satellite map of Johnson Harbor. It was just a hundred miles north. Jonah must have been close this whole time, waiting to make a break for it.

Philip went into the bathroom and changed into his day clothes, brushed his teeth and slicked back his hair. When he came out of the bathroom he saw Darcy of all things sitting at the little breakfast table by the window looking at his laptop, imagine that. She turned and looked at him with still sleepy eyes.

"Johnson Harbor, I've been there. Are you going for a visit?"

Philip went to his bag by the bed and turned his back to her as he pulled out the pistol and twisted the silencer onto the barrel.

"I really wish you would've stayed in bed love."

At the front of the hotel he got into a cab that was parked near the lobby. "Airport please," he instructed the driver. He needed to borrow a helicopter quick.

29.

Barton hung up the phone and continued looking out the window with the binoculars when he heard a noise and turned to see that Cree Johnson was standing in the doorway. He just about jumped backwards at the sight of Cree's tattooed face and fierce eyes. And now there was something more terrible and frightening in those bloodshot eyes.

"How long have you been standing there?" asked Barton, his voice trembled against his will.

"Long enough," Cree flatly replied in a low voice. "What have you done?" It was as much a statement as a question and he didn't wait for a reply as he slowly closed and locked the door behind him without taking his eyes off of Barton.

"Don't you come near me." Barton yelled and fumbled for the phone and dropped it on the ground as Cree quickly closed the distance between them.

Jonah was inspecting the bolts that held the broken pontoon to the plane, getting ready in his mind for replacing it as quickly as possible and getting back in the air. Abby and the others were sitting on the end of the pontoon relishing the morning sun and the fact that they had survived the harrowing landing.

Cree came jogging up from the harbor masters house and pulled Jonah to the side and whispered in his ear.

Jonah's face turned grim. "So you're certain what you heard?"

"Oh yeah, he was telling someone on the other end of the line who we were and where we were, and looking for a reward for the telling of it. Said it was a reporter who called him last week looking for clues to you and your planes disappearance, he also said some other people had called asking if anyone had seen the plane, but this guy was the only one offering a reward and so he called him first. Money grubbing bastard!" Cree spit on the ground.

"Where's Barton now?"

"I hog tied him so he couldn't cause any more trouble until we figured out what to do. Put up a bit of fight." He rubbed his jaw. "But I got him. What do you think? It could have been legit, a reporter looking for a story?"

Jonah shook his head.

"We can't take that chance. The nearest airport is less than a hundred miles away. A fast helicopter can get here in twenty minutes. It'll take at least an hour to switch out the pontoons, minimum, and then there are problems we could encounter. Those pontoons are in the water all the time, salt water at that, the bolts could be frozen and we'd need a blow torch to remove them, we might have to jerry rig a spare part or two. It'll take an hour minimum, if everything goes smooth, and now since our cover has been blown that hour is too long and too risky. We have to get out of here, now."

They talked in hushed tones back and forth and finally Jonah nodded in agreement with what Cree was advising.

Jonah walked back towards his passengers. "Alright change of plans Abby, we'll all go into town together and get George and Harold to the Doctors office and then come back for our little repair."

"There's Pop, right on time," said Cree as an old station wagon came into view, Cree had called him from the harbor masters house after tying up Barton. The old man driving pulled up next to them and got out. He was a carbon copy of Cree, but older and greyer and bent from age, and the lines in his face deeper and longer, but he had the same Indian look, serious and fierce, with a twinkle of mirth at the corners of his eyes.

He went straight to Jonah and shook his hand and gave a big hug. "My son has returned," he said and held him at arm's length looked long and studied his face. "You haven't changed a bit Jonah."

"Thanks Pop, it's great to see you. This is my friend Abby," as he motioned to her. "And our passengers George, and Harold."

The old man held his palm up in greeting. "Yes I met George and Harold last week on their way to the mountains." He winked at Harold. "So you had trouble with your aim, eh?" and then started walking back to the station wagon, "We'd better get you to the Doctor right away before he heads out to go fishing on this fine Sunday morning. I see his boat is still tied up at the dock but we'd better hurry."

They all piled into the wagon, and it took off in a trail of dust towards the town. Doctor Miller's office was a little cottage on Main Street with a white picket fence, big front porch, double doors at the entrance, and served double duty as a house and hospital.

Dr. Miller stood on the porch with a cup of coffee in his hand waiting for them. Jonah and Cree half carried and half dragged Harold up the stairs and into the waiting room, sitting him down in a cushioned chair. He was still groggy from the pain pills he'd taken only a few hours before, and winced as he sat down.

Cree did not like going to the Doctor one bit, and in fact considered it bad luck to even be on the street. But, business was business and when one of his charges got injured which happened more frequently than he would admit, to the little cottage he would go and then get out as quickly as possible.

"Well, thanks again for going on the Wild Indian Adventure Tour," he said to Harold and headed for the door with a nod at Dr. Miller as he passed. "Morning Doc."

"Good morning Cree."

Cree's hand was on the doorknob when Harold blurted, "Aren't you gonna stay and see what the Doc says?"

"I'll check back with him some other day, I'm almost certain I'll be back." and he rushed out the door.

Cree's family house was on the very south side of the little town and set high on a knoll that looked out over the ocean and the harbor.

On a clear night they could see the glow from the city lights of Vancouver Island. It was an old house handed down through the generation, and even though it was over a hundred years old it always had a fresh coat of paint. Cree liked to joke that the nails had rusted long before he was born, and the paint was the only thing holding the house together.

There was a swing set out front and little bikes leaning against the porch. If Abby was in a better mood she would have thought it was a perfect home to raise a family. But now it was just a way station on their journey to another place to hide. She sat gloomily in a chair on the porch while Cree went inside and began gathering supplies. He unlocked a cabinet and brought out boxes of bullets and stacked them on the counter.

Jonah went to the phone hanging on the wall. It was an old rotary model from another era of time, black and shiny and made of metal. He dialed a nine digit long distance number to his boss, using the circular wheel, each number taking an eternity as it clackety clacked back into place.

The phone on the other end rang five times and then a woman's voice answered. Her voice was small and thin. "Hello?"

"Connie this is Jonah."

There was a long pause on the other end, and then, "Jonah, my God where are you?"

He thought he heard a dim clicking sound and knew the line would be tapped, but at this point it didn't matter.

"I'll explain later, right now I need to talk to Ross."

He heard soft sobbing on the other end and then, "He's dead Jonah. He died of a heart attack the day you left." Her sobbing eased and she took a deep breath. "They said you had a nervous breakdown Jonah, that you killed the guard, destroyed the lab in a fit of rage and kidnapped Abby. They found a note they say you wrote at the lab. Ross didn't believe it, and neither did I. He was driving to the lab to meet with the police, but he never made it. They found him parked on the side of the road, half a mile from the lab."

Jonah narrowed his eyes. Ross was the only other person in the world who knew what they had created. He was in top shape, jogged two miles every day, and had just competed in a marathon. There were however many ways to make an unnatural death appear to be natural.

"It's not true Connie, none of it. What about the surveillance cameras, the tapes?"

"They were all blank Jonah. They said you must have deliberately erased them. All the files are gone Jonah, all the research files wiped out in the fire, even the backup servers."

"Connie, I have to go. I'm sorry about Ross; you know he was like a brother to me, my big brother. I'll be home soon and we'll sort this all out."

He hung up the phone as she continued to talk, the click of the phone as it settled in the cradle ending the call. So that was it. They staged the whole thing, killed Penny and Win, killed Ross, burned the lab, took the research files, and framed him. Bastards.

He walked back onto the porch. Cree had a pile of gear on the step and was loading it into the station wagon. Pop Johnson was talking in low tones to Abby asking her all about her life. A smile had permeated her being again as she conversed with the old man, and life took on a normal feeling for the moment.

Off in the distance to the south along the coast very dim at first, barely audible and then gaining in strength they heard the thump, thump, thump from a helicopter. It was too low on the horizon and there were too many trees obscuring the southern coastline, but the sound was unmistakable.

They all stopped what they were doing and stood still, listening and watching, and then it came into view travelling fast about a hundred feet off the ocean, tilted forward for maximum acceleration was a small red helicopter.

"It's a forest service copter," said Cree.

Abby stood slowly, her voice was hopeful. "Maybe it's on forest service business, official business. Maybe they're here to help."

Jonah put his hand on Abby's shoulder to support her. "I just got off the phone with Ross's wife. He's dead, the lab was burned to the ground, all the files are gone and they found a note that says I did it."

The sense of normalcy was gone, replaced by a feeling of utter dread. The blood drained out of Abby's face and she turned ash white as the realization seeped in. The helicopter didn't hold people that were here to help; they held people that were here to hurt. The fast moving red helicopter was suddenly an angry omen of impending destruction. It circled the harbor below, the thump of the rotors suddenly loud and powerful and echoing off the walls of the porch, and it landed in a whirlwind of dust that rose in the air.

"Time to go," said Cree.

30.

Barton was tied up in the far corner of the harbor masters house. He was seated in the swivel chair with a hundred coils of rope around his body knotted in all types of specialty knots, bow lines and square knots and clove hitches and sheet bends. A rag was stuffed in his mouth and duct taped around his head, and he could barely whimper out a sound. The chair was hitched to the old metal heater and he couldn't move an inch. His head hurt from the punch that sent him unconscious and his arms hurt from the pummeling that took place prior to the knock out. One thing was certain in his mind was that as soon as he got out of this predicament he'd get the marshal over from town and have Cree thrown in jail for the rest of eternity.

He heard the thump of the helicopter approaching, and then deafening sound as it landed nearby. Whoever in the hell is flying that thing was really pushing the limit he thought, almost like a military operation in a combat zone with the helicopter swooping in at full speed to take out the enemy.

Hey, maybe that's it, he thought. Maybe someone on the outside knew he was in trouble and had come to rescue him. Heck, he hadn't even had time to call the police and let them know that Jonahs' bush plane had landed here. He'd barely had time to cover himself before that damn Indian ambushed him and knocked him cold.

The front doorknob made a sound, like someone was on the outside turning it and trying to open the door; the only door to the outside, but it was locked. He tried to make a sound, to let them know he was in here, but all that came out was a muffled grunt. He tried to shake the chair he was in but it was shackled so tightly to the metal grate and he was so laden down with thick rope that not a sound was made. He could see the shadow of someone looking through the window but the shades were so thick and dirty that whoever was on the outside would have had an impossible time seeing his rope laden shape way off in this dark corner of the room.

He heard the door knob again, and this time there was a different kind of noise coming from it, and he could see a thin metal blade inch its way along the door jamb next to the knob and the door suddenly opened. In stepped a man with slick black hair carrying a briefcase and he surveyed the scene and quickly closed the door behind him.

"My good fellow," he exclaimed. "What the heck has happened here?"

Barton tried to speak and out came a muffled grunt and his face turned red as he tried to shout.

The well dressed man hurried over to him and pulled the tape off Barton's head, pulling some hair in the process. He plucked the rag out his mouth and Barton took some deep breaths, coughed out some phlegm and spoke.

"Those bastards! I'll have their heads for this." He looked up at the man with the slick black hair and the slight scar on his cheek. He looked strange, Caucasian features but with dark skin and slick straight hair that was too black. Barton being the racist that he was barked a command at the perceived subhuman. "Well what the hell are you waiting for? Untie me buddy!"

"I'll untie you if you answer some questions."

"What, who are you?"

"Who am I? Who the hell are you to be rude to someone who just took a gag out of your mouth? Should I put it back?"

Barton winced. He was a big man with a square jaw, well fed like a lumberjack, and this subhuman was small by comparison, in fact Barton imagined he could crush him if got the chance, but the gag scared him.

"Alright, alright, thank you for helping me, I'm Barton O'Conner. I own this harbor, and most of the town."

"Now you see? That's how to be polite. I'm John Mack?"

"The reporter? Why didn't you say so in the first place?"

"Well, it's not often that you come across someone tied up in the corner like this, even in my business."

"Speaking of that, do you think you could

untie me? Please?"

"Oh, right." The first knot was right on Barton's chest and it would not come undone. A switchblade clicked open and he began slicing away the ropes. Barton wondered briefly why a man wearing a suit and tie would be carrying a switchblade. Within seconds, Barton was free. He stood up and stretched and felt his jaw where Cree had nearly broken it, but it felt intact.

"You look different than I expected," said Barton, towering over the other man. "Say, how'd you get here so quickly? We only talked on the phone about a half hour ago."

"You have to be quick in this business, speaking of which, let's get down to it. Where did the people from that bush plane go?"

Barton was feeling big and bad and obnoxious again. "How the hell should I know? One of 'em, that dirty bastard Indian known as Cree busted in here and tied me up.

Caught me by surprise, otherwise I woulda whupped him good."

"So, you were on the phone to me when he busted in?"

"Yeah, how'd you know? I hung up the phone and he snuck up on me. Caught me from behind like the dirty sneakin' Indian that he is."

Philip Weintraub knew instantly what had happened. The Indian Cree had caught Barton talking with him and tied him up to keep him from calling anyone else.

"Did you hear another plane, or helicopter

take off after they tied you up?"

"Naw, it's been quiet."

"Any idea where they could have gone? Does Cree have house here?"

"Sure he's got a house, on the south side of town. You can't miss it; he's got a damn teepee on the front lawn."

Philip knew they would be long gone from there, but he would check it out as soon as he was finished with Barton.

"Any hiding places you can think of that they might have gone to?"

"Sure, there's millions of 'em, all over the hills."

"C'mon, think man, there must be someplace they would go to in a crisis."

Barton had had enough of this. He frowned at Philip. "Yeah, well it's about time I call the cops." He started towards the phone on the desk and felt a hand on his wrist. This little guy looked weak but his grip was like a vise. Barton took a step back and rubbed his wrist.

"Hey, what's the deal?"

"Just another minute and we'll be done and then you can call the cops, okay?"

"Sure pal, whatever you say."

Philip pulled out a laptop and placed in on the desk. He scrolled through a series of folders and then opened one up and clicked onto a file. It was filled with wide angle photos of the interior of an office, a desk with chairs and walls with framed pictures, a pool table, dartboard, punching bag, it was the interior of Jonah's office captured in High Definition photos from the fly on the wall bugging device.

Philip zoomed in on a wall and scrolled sideways. "Take a good look and tell me if any of these places look familiar."

Barton frowned, ticked off at this delay. "Alright, I'll play along."

The scene on the computer screen showed Jonah and assorted others in the wilderness holding up trophy fish for the camera, smiling, sometimes hamming it up and clowning around for the camera covered in rain, or mud to their wastes.

"Anything?"

Barton shook his head and answered impatiently. "These could be anywhere, I mean c'mon buddy, a round lake? A stream with trees in the background? There's gazillions of spots like these all over the world."

"Sure, sure, keep looking please."

The scene kept scrolling sideways. Jonah on a podium accepting an award, a diploma, another award, more fishing.

"Hold it," Barton commanded.

There was an old faded photo of Jonah standing on a rock in the middle of a stream with a middle aged but grey haired man at his side that looked just like him but older. The older man was holding up a large salmon, and smiling from ear to ear. Behind him was a towering waterfall, and filling the frame to the right was the steep side of a round mountain void of vegetation.

"Yeah, I know this place."

"Good."

"They call it the hole in the wall. Damned hard to get to. The Indians say you have to be half mountain goat to get into that valley."

"Where's it at?"

"About twenty miles straight east. There's an old logging road that runs along the edge of the mountain, I can show you on a map."

"I'm not driving."

"Oh right. Well, I've told you all I know, so unless there's some more pictures…"

Philip scrolled sideways and the screen showed the first wall that they started with. "No I guess that's it."

Barton arched his eyebrows and motioned towards the phone with his hand. "Well if you don't mind, I'd like to call the police so I report being assaulted and tied up."

"Yes, about that…" Philip said as he reached into his briefcase and pulled out the pistol. The silencer was still attached to the barrel, and he'd reloaded back at the hotel.

31.

The station wagon was loaded up, Cree was at the wheel and cranked the engine, white smoke bellowed from the exhaust as Abby and Jonah crowded into the front seat next to him. Pops was standing next to the driver side window and put his hand on Cree's arm.

"Be strong my warrior son. I pray to the Great Spirit that I'll see you again."

Cree nodded. "Don't worry Pop, we'll be gone for a few days, maybe a few weeks, whatever it takes. I've got the short wave radio so you call if you need to get in touch with me."

"Just stay hidden in the bosom of the wild till the danger passes."

"You too, eh?"

Pops just chuckled. "Don't you worry about me! If your Grandma couldn't find my hideout after all those years of trying…" His voice trailed off and he stared into the distant sky.

Cree squeezed Pops hand one last time and then pulled away from the little house slowly at first down the dirt road leading east through the forest and then floored the gas pedal and the wagon barreled down the road.

Pop watched the car disappear into the distance in a ball of dust and gravel, and then he walked high up into the forest and wrapped himself in a blanket of branches and leaves at the base of a sycamore on a hill that overlooked the town and waited.

About ten minutes later he heard the sound of the helicopter taking off from the harbor and it looped over the town and hovered over the house and then landed in a clearing by the driveway near the teepee. The engine wound down and a man leapt out of the cockpit and ran towards the tree line next to the house.

Pop got out his binoculars and followed the man as he blended into the greenery and then lost him.

He panned over to the little house, and he focused the binoculars on the front door. The man flew out of the bushes up onto the porch, and burst through the front door holding a pistol in front of him and disappeared into the house. Pop watched and waited scanning the exterior of the home, and now and then catching a glimpse through the windows. The man was searching the house.

After a while he reappeared through the front door and stood on the porch looking out onto the surrounding area, and at one point seemed to be looking right at Pop, who stayed as still as he could, hidden in his cloak of pine branches.

Pop could see the little scar running down the side of the man's cheekbone, and the serious look on his face. There was no fear in those eyes, and they reminded Pop of a wolf's eyes when it is hunting and hungry.

Then the man walked down to the driveway and knelt down on his hands and knees and studied the tire tracks. He followed the distinctive track from the town, and then walked out onto the dirt road way and saw how the same tracks went off into the East towards the mountains. The man then ran over and jumped into the helicopter and the engine wound back up with a high pitched whine, and the rotors beat the air with steadily increasing speed until it lifted off the ground and headed towards the mountains slowly following the dirt road.

Pop waited until the red chopper was well out of sight and then he climbed out of his cloak and continued on into the forest towards his hideout.

Soon he was safe in the nook of the canyon in the shelter he'd built with his own hands fifty years before. It was nestled against a sheer cliff under an outcrop of rock that protected him from the boulders that occasionally fell, and he camouflaged the entrance with native mosses and trees.

When he was certain he was safe and no one had followed him he pulled out the two way short wave radio and powered it up and called for Cree.

Normally an amateur or ham radio operator will have a specific call sign with designated letters and numbers issued by the feds. Pop could never remember his so he always began with a simple, "ABC123 over." He repeated it twice, "ABC123 over," and then waited.

The static of the radio crackled in the car as Cree barreled down the highway on a straightaway, the speedometer read eighty five.

Jonah grabbed the radio from the dashboard and answered for Cree.

"ABC123 go ahead."

"Son?"

Static.

"Yes, over."

"One man, average build, scar on his cheek, with a handgun, flying now your way."

And then Pop remembered protocol. "Over."

Cree turned to Jonah. "Is that your guy?"

"Yeah," said Jonah.

Jonah clicked the transmit button on the radio, "ABC123, roger that, now go to ground, repeat, go to ground. Over."

They heard the double click in their receiver as Pop signed off on the other end and Cree punched the gas pedal to the floor.

"We have to get off the road," said Cree and he searched for a place to pull over.

"What's our plan Jonah?" asked Cree.

"Hide."

"And then what?"

"Yes, and then what," said Cree. "They'll never stop coming after you."

"We have the short wave radio, it's untraceable," said Jonah. "We'll get to the hole in the wall and then we'll start making calls. We'll call everyone, newspapers, police, FBI, I don't know, but we need to get our story out there, get the word out, get to someone who can help us. But in the meantime we need to stay alive."

The car careened around a bend in the road and a logging truck was heading straight for them hogging the whole road, the trucker leaned on the horn and the sound of it blasted throughout the forest, Cree slammed on the brakes and cranked the wheel sending the station wagon crashing into the bushes and it came to a halt inches from a giant redwood.

Cree backed out of the bushes and the trucker looked in his rear view mirror as he slowed down, and seeing that they were okay blasted his horn again and kept on going down the road, still hogging the whole thing.

Cree cursed and shook his fist out the window at the departing truck. "Crazy bastard!"

"What were you saying about staying alive?" asked Jonah.

"Oh yeah, we need to stay alive."

Abby let out a sigh of relief.

"This is as good as anywhere," said Cree and he maneuvered around the big redwood and found a break in the forest and pulled the station wagon well into the woods and into an alcove of branches and leaves. "Quickly now," he said and jumped out the wagon with a machete and began chopping branches and throwing them towards Abby. "Pile them on top of the car."

Jonah ran back towards the dirt road with one of the branches and carefully swept the dirt to mask their path and then arranged some more leaves and natural debris on the way back to the car in the shadows.

They were near the mountain they called the Old Man. Its bald top showed through the tops of the trees and towered above the dirt road.

"We walk from here," said Cree.

They unloaded the back packs and rifles and lay them on the side and began covering the station wagon with more branches. Cree took the machete and went deep into the forest and came back with armfuls of green bushes.

Soon the car was completely camouflaged, and indistinguishable from the surrounding forest. He took out three camouflage hats and shirts from the backpack and tossed one pair each to the others. "Put these on." Then he pulled out two small metal canisters and after dipping his two fingers into the goo painted his face and hands with black and green streaks.

"Like this," he told them, and held the canisters while they dipped their fingers. Finally satisfied, Cree shouldered his backpack and slung his rifle and checked the chamber with a clack.

Jonah and Abby did the same, Abby's backpack was a bit smaller than Cree and Jonah's, but the rifle was the same caliber and she also checked the chamber with a definitive move. "Let's hope we won't need these," she said.

Cree's face was steady as he looked upwards towards the Old Man. "Hope is for children and old ones," he said. "We must be ready."

The quiet of the forest suddenly overwhelmed them and Cree began to lead them towards the mountain.

They'd only taken a few steps when they heard the faint sound of a helicopter far in the distance. It seemed to be headed their way but it was hard to tell. When you are deep in a forest near a mountain where sounds bounce like a trampoline, the pop of a helicopter's rotor when it is flying low in a searching pattern seem to be coming from all directions, loud and then soft and disappearing altogether like the craft fell into a hole, and then reappearing much louder then soft again in a rotating medley of volume.

Cree looked at Jonah. "You're the pilot, what do you think?"

"Gas turbine, small engine."

"Like the one at the harbor."

"Could be, you hear that distinctive pop?"

"Yeah."

Jonah nodded. "It could be the same one. Anyways, we'll know soon enough because here it comes."

The medley of sounds suddenly got very loud and they could see glimpses of the red helicopter through the trees following the road, the sound of the rotor now a steady pop pop pop. They instinctively crouched under a thicket of branches as the helicopter swept by and out of sight.

"He's looking for us," said Abby.

"You think he's following our tire tracks?"

asked Jonah.

"Too many tracks on that road to follow, but I tell you it is lucky that they are running the logging trucks today or else we would be found." The steady pop of the rotor went back to the medley of dim and absent and semi loud pops and seemed to go over a ridge and disappear.

They moved quickly now through the forest and the ground began to slope upwards and the going got tougher. Abby was breathing hard and sweat was pouring down her face. She stopped and leaned against a tree to catch her breath. Jonah was pulling up the rear and he gave a little bird whistle to stop Cree who was powering up the hill. A quarter mile away and in front of them was a majestic five hundred foot waterfall that cascaded down a huge cliff face. The sunlight danced through the trees and created a perpetual rainbow with the mist at the base where the water crashed into the stream.

"I've never seen anything so incredible in my life..." said Abby between gulps of air.

"It's about to get real fun," said Jonah with a wry smile.

"What do you mean?"

"You see that cliff?"

"Yes."

"We're going up it."

"Surely you're kidding." She bit her lower lip and scanned the cliff face for a route up. The sheer wall of the cliff butted up against the Old Man on one side, the Old Woman on the other, and in the middle side fell straight off in a stair step of smaller cliffs that ended at the stream bed.

"We found the way up when we were kids." He grinned. "You know, the young and crazy type."

They climbed for an hour up through moss and lichen covered crevices, cracks in the rock wall dripping with moisture from the falls. They paused at a level spot and drank from their canteens.

The waterfall spilled into a pool nearby, pausing and then continued over the cliff. "The water looks so clean and clear," she remarked.

"Never trust it," said Cree. "Not with a flow this big. There could be a dead antelope, or bear in the water just upstream."

She winced. "I'll stick with the canteen water," and took another drink. "How much farther?" she asked.

Cree measured the distance remaining to the top. "About another hour, we're almost there."

He pointed to a large sandstone rock in a hollow nearby. Carved on the face of it were the initials CJ and below that JM.

Cree looked angry. "Dang kids tagging the rocks up here."

"Vandals", said Jonah.

Abby nodded her concurrence, "I hate graffiti". Then she noticed the wry looks and realized she'd been had. "Hey, those are your initials."

The men laughed, and then they continued up the crevices towards the top.

"Dang kids is right," muttered Abby as she continued after them.

The sun was setting low on the western horizon as they made their way over the last ledge and there, stretched in front of them was a Shangri-la valley winding between the mountains into the darkness.

"Let's find a place to camp for the night," said Cree and he led them to a small clearing near the stream. They found a semi flat spot and set up the tarp. Cree pulled out the satellite phone from the bottom of his backpack and set it on a rock. "I should have brought this with me on the hunt with the car salesmen, and then you two would still be safe and sound on the lake."

"Not safe," said Jonah.

"You want to use it now, call some newspapers, police, and give them your side of the story?"

"Not yet. These satellite phones can be triangulated, tracked. We'll wait."

Cree looked at the deepening gloom of the valley. "We're already being tracked."

32.

Philip flew above the logging road towards the mountains. Down below he studied the dirt road, the intricate weave of tire tracks winding through the dust and mud. The logging trucks that were scattered along the way were leaving deep and wide tracks, and it looked like there were smaller tracks interspersed among them but it was too hard to tell. He continued searching as he flew, but now concentrated on the future. He was fast approaching the mountains and the waterfalls that flowed between them from the hanging valley. The logging road turned and wound back towards the coast around the Old Woman and away from the bald mountain, and he hovered for a moment at the big curve, studying the tracks again. It was useless, they all looked the same. He knew they would hide their car in the woods and hike into the wilderness, and try to disappear; they could already be on foot for all he knew.

Philip's mind was made up now. He would fly into the hanging valley and find a place to land somewhere on the opposite side or on a ridge and hike towards them, hunting them. He took a left turn and flew not straight towards the valley, but around the Old Woman Mountain so he could come in from the opposite side, for if they were observing him they would think he was heading away and along the logging road and that they were safe. He wanted them to think they were safe.

He came around the back side of the Old Woman and found the spot he was looking for. Down below was a small clearing near the second waterfall that spilled into the hanging valley. He settled the chopper down onto the grassy turf and turned off the engine and it wound slowly down to silence. He grabbed the packs and gear from the back seats and arranged it all on the forest floor. The camouflage gear he'd taken from Cree's house was a little big and he duct taped the ankles so that it didn't drag on the ground. He used the hunting knife to cut the sleeves shorter, and finally satisfied he got out the green and black face paint and smeared it in lines across his cheeks and forehead, and hands and forearms, and then he checked his guns and ammo, locking the bullets in the chambers and latching the safeties on the triggers. The long rifle went into an oiled sling and the handguns went into his waist bands. He tied the camouflage hat onto his head and with his eyes now wild like his surrounding darting under the brow of the hat he crept silently into the shadows and through the forest.

When he got to the edge of the valley he pulled out his binoculars and searched the area below him. It wasn't a huge valley, only about three miles long and a half mile wide filled with forest and a wide stream running through the middle of it. He was about a thousand feet above the valley and steep walls like a bowl protected the entrance to the valley. To his left was the top of waterfall and the Old Man, the bald mountain towering above him. To the right was the Old Woman, the forest covered mountain also towering above him with its steep hills careening down like an avalanche of living pine to the valley floor. He studied all the walls of the valley and then made his decision on which angle to take. He began picking his way to the right and down the tangled mash of forest and undergrowth at the feet of the Old Woman.

It was getting dark and there was no sense stumbling around attracting attention and so he found two trees that were growing right next to each other and climbed twenty feet into the air.

He stood on a sturdy branch and leaned over to the adjacent tree and tied the end of a rope to a branch, and then tied the other end to the tree he was standing on. In between the ends of the rope was a woven hammock and after tying his pack to the tree he was standing on, he opened the hammock and eased into it.

He checked his watch, it was eleven thirty so it would be light again in about four hours, enough time to catch some rest and get ready for the events of the day. Tomorrow he would search the valley from one end to the other, slowly, methodically, quietly and invisibly, or as much as humanly possible. He hadn't been on a hunt like this for a long time and if he must admit it, he was looking forward to it. As someone who counts sheep to help getting to sleep, he thought back two years ago to another great hunt.

He had been sent to Kazakhstan to take out a troublemaking warlord causing grief to the sheik's profit margin. The warlord escaped the trap Philip had set for him in the city and fled to the mountains on horseback with a couple of his lieutenants for protection. It was a great battle of wits in the wilds near the Kungey Alatau Mountains in the central part of the country, which in fact looked much like the country they were in now with tall forest covered mountains, streams and lakes. The time of year was different though and they fought in the darkness of winter in the freezing snow. This was almost like being on vacation compared to that time.

He remembered as he was drifting off to sleep the fear he saw in the warlord's face as he put the bullets into his forehead, and he smiled as he fell asleep, the wind gently whispering in the tall pines and the water flowing in the stream below in the valley.

33.

Abby whispered. "What do you mean we're being tracked?"

"Just an instinct," said Cree. "I am a hunter after all by trade; I hunt animals, and I know what the feeling is like. And I have been hunted myself at times, by wolves, grizzlies, hungry animals tracking me. One time when I was young and stupid and I was hiking on a trail near our house, I had a peculiar feeling that I was being followed and I kept looking around to see who it was. I thought it might have been Barton ready to jump out at me to get back at me for something I'd done to him. And then I saw this big mountain lion hidden in the bushes, his eyes watching me, stalking me. Have you ever seen a mountain lion in the wild?"

Abby shook her head.

"He was about two hundred pounds of cat, and he slid out of the bushes and down onto the trail. I didn't dare run and so I tried to stare it down for a little while. It just stood there and stared back, it looked hungry, and then I started walking slowly down the trail backwards, keeping my eyes on it, and it began following me about a hundred feet back. I'd never been so scared in my life, and never as much since. I knew it wanted to eat me."

Abby asked, "Didn't you have a gun?"

"No gun, I was ten. After a while I came across a big stick that was about the size of a baseball bat and I picked it up. I knew it wouldn't help me against that big cat but maybe I could get in a swing or two before it got me. He crept off into the bushes above the trail and disappeared. I walked as fast as I could and then ran home. I remember the hackles on the back of my neck standing on end the whole way. It's the last time I ever went hiking without a gun."

The darkness settled in around them and they were silent and then Cree started again. "It's kind of strange, but you know that feeling that I had with my neck hairs standing on end? I never had that feeling again, until now. And now I even have a gun with me."

"You're scaring Abby," said Jonah.

Her eyes were steady. "It's okay, I can take it," she said.

"It's not my purpose, to scare anyone," said Cree. "Maybe it's just my hunter's instinct kicking in, and I want you both to know what it is that I sense. We're in this together."

"After what I've been through the past couple of days," said Abby, "I'm tired of running, tired of hiding, tired of being scared. I'm just plain tired. I want this to be over so I can go back to a normal life. I want to go back to a home with hot running water and a shower, and a soft bed with a pillow, and I want to sleep throughout the night without wondering if something is going to jump out of the bushes at me. I want to go back to the lab and invent something, cure cancer, or the common cold or anything for that matter. I want to live again without looking over my shoulder. But I know that's not going to happen until we settle this business, and so right now I'm hoping this creep, or creeps really are here in this valley with us and we can get the jump on him, or them, or however many there may be."

Jonah sat motionless. He knew that they would never be able to go back to a normal life, not now. Not with what they knew, what they had in their possession, and what they could do with it.

"She's right," said Cree, "we need to set a trap. I'll come up with a plan."

They slept for a few short hours, Cree and Jonah taking turns watching over the party. When the slight bit of light began to creep over the mountains, they gently woke Abby and made their way deeper in the valley.

If you took twenty football stadiums and put them end to end you would have the shape of the valley. A quarter mile wide and five miles long, it was filled with pine, birch, cedar, maple and oak trees, and with a strong running stream that meandered through the middle with whirlpools and rapids and calm areas, filled with native trout and the seasonal Pacific salmon that travelled up the waterfalls and rapids in the late summer months to spawn.

The Old Woman guarded one side of the valley, and the Old Man the other. Both mountains came straight down to the level valley floor that was somewhat level from an ancient flood.

They crept through the undergrowth keeping a watchful eye as they went and careful not to so much as step on a branch or stir a rock to make a sound. Cree led them through the valley towards the steep cliff face that led from the floor of the valley up the side of the Old Man.

It was still semi dark in the valley, but high up on the bald mountain the light of the coming dawn shone bright on the treeless peak.

"This is where we'll make our stand," said Cree. "We'll have our backs to the wall and will only have one side to defend. Jonah, you and Abby will stay on this lower step and hide in the underbrush at the base of the old man. There are small caves and cracks where you can be safe. I'll go up high and find a place with a vantage point and when the hunter comes towards this area as I'm sure he will, I'll shoot him dead."

"It sounds like we're the bait," said Abby.

"There are no trees up on the Old Man," said Cree. "Nowhere to hide. I might only have one shot, maybe two. I'll find a place up there and try to blend in to the rocks; I'll find a ledge or an overhang where I can set up a shot. It's our best chance I think, much better than being in the middle of the valley with four sides to defend against. This isn't like hunting a deer or a bear, where I could circle the valley and flank him at will. This is a man, and an unknown one at that, and we don't what type of training he has, and so we have to wait for him to make the first move. This our best bet with what we have."

"It's a trap," said Jonah. "For him, and hopefully not for us."

A thick line of brush and trees ringed the base of the mountain, and then thinned out towards the stream. Cree led the way and found a nook in the rocks where he instructed Abby to hide where she'd be able to see through a crack in the rocks and the brush to the valley, and then he positioned Jonah to her left where he had a straight shot to the valley through the trees. He stepped back to make sure they blended in with the brush.

"I'll be right above you, about a hundred feet up," he said. "I see a little ledge that I hide on top of."

There was a myriad of birds singing in the morning throughout the forest, sparrows and warblers and doves flew from tree to tree singing a song or two before moving on, searching for bugs and friends, and sometimes just singing to hear their own songs.

"I'll give a little whistle when I'm in position, and another when I see him," said Cree. "Like this," and he whistled softly like a sparrow. "And then you be ready." He began climbing the steep rocky side of the mountain with his rifle slung over his shoulder. Now and then a small pebble would come tumbling down the side and they covered their heads, and after a while all was quiet, and they heard the first whistle.

Time went slowly by and the sun rose higher in the sky filling the valley. It was still and hot and they could hear the gentle rustling of the stream in the distance.

Abby quietly opened a canteen and took a sip of water and motioned it towards Jonah. He waved it off and kept his watch towards the valley cradling the rifle in his arms and his finger just off the trigger.

The day wore on, hour after hour and still no second whistle from above. The sun had passed overhead and was now on its way down towards evening. They had seen a lot of wildlife pass by their hide out and so they knew they were invisible in the bush. A family of deer had walked nearby, the doe and its fawn grazing as the buck kept a close watch, a cute little porcupine wandered lazily a couple of feet away and sniffed the air and then hustled down the valley.

There were birds everywhere throughout the valley, and their singing filled the air.

"How are we going to be able to tell if it's Cree whistling?" she asked.

Jonah craned his head to the side, and listened carefully.

"They're only in the trees," he said, "I don't hear any up on the mountain above us."

Abby stretched her legs, and cursed a little under her breath as she nursed a cramp in one of her calves.

They were nearly lulled to sleep by the peace of the valley, and then it came. A single faint whistle from a sparrow from above, and any thought of a gentle nap was replaced by a sudden gut wrench, and they waited for the man with the scar to appear.

Jonah had been leaning back on a flat rock, and now he sat straight up and aimed his gun towards the valley, still keeping his finger off the trigger so he wouldn't accidently pull it and give away their position.

Abby left hand began shaking slightly and she reached over with her right to steady it. The rifle lay across her lap and she was afraid to pick it up.

An eternity passed and then the sound of the rifle above them fired a shot, and a moment later a second shot from above and it echoed in the valley. And then silence for a moment, then from down in the valley three quick pops from another gun, and then silence as those sounds echoed from mountain to mountain and down through the valley.

First one pebble, and then another, and then a shower of pebbles came down from above and then a terrible cracking of branches as Cree's body fell from the sky and crumpled in a heap on the rocks in front of them.

Abby looked away. Jonah whispered to her, "We have to go," and he reached out and pulled at her arm, "quick now."

They hugged the rock wall and crept through the brush away from Cree's body, and when they had gone about a hundred yards they came across an old dry stream bed that fed down into the main stream in the wet months. It was cut low in the valley and filled with rocks from the mountain, and they ran along it until they were far away from where Cree had fallen. They made their way to the edge of the stream and crouched behind a large boulder beside a calm pool.

"We have to get out of this valley as quick as possible," said Jonah. "We'll ride the stream down as far as the waterfall and then take the cliff trail out."

He was climbing down into the stream when the bullet hit him high in the chest right above his heart. His face turned white and he wheezed to her, "Run." And then he fell head first into the pool.

Abby grabbed his feet and tried to wrestle him back out of the water but he was too heavy. Precious seconds went by as he lay motionless under the water, she grabbed him by the collar of his shirt and managed to get his head out of the water for a moment and then her foot slipped on a rock and down he went again. She held onto a rock on the bank and strained to lift him out of the pool. It was impossible and so she dragged him through the water towards the shallow portion of the stream where she could get more leverage. He had been under water for close to a minute now and time was running out.

"I'm not leaving you," she cried.

The cold barrel of a gun touched her face as

she strained with Jonah, and she turned to see the man with the scar kneeling beside her, the pistol in his hand jet black and the hollow barrel pointed right between her eyes. His left arm was hanging lifeless at his side and his shirt at the shoulder was stained with fresh blood.

"Well now isn't this touching?" said Philip.

He put his face inches away from hers and grinned. She could smell his sour breath and sweat.

"Say love," he asked her, "how about we do something fun tonight? I'm new in town and you can show me around, you know have some dinner, see a movie...." He laughed a hideous laugh, saliva dripping from his lips.

She could feel her left hand on a round stone the size of a baseball at the bottom of the stream and she circled her fingers around it holding it tight, and then brought it up quick and smashed it into Philips face, and he shuddered with shock and fell back on the rocks and hit his head knocking him unconscious. She dropped the rock and was able to pull Jonah up so that his face was out of the water in the shallows and she started CPR. He wasn't responding, and the stream was pulling at him again and she was running out of strength to hold him back. She pulled him farther out of the water onto the rocks, and went back to her training, fifteen compressions, two respirations over and over, fifteen compressions, two respirations, but he wasn't responding, he wasn't responding, and tears flowed down her cheeks as she pumped his chest.

"Please don't leave me Jonah, don't leave me."

Philip moaned and then wheezed and began to wake up, rolling his head from side to side on the ground, blood streaming from his mouth where she'd smashed the rock.

Abby leapt towards him and tried to get the gun out of his hand but his grip was too strong and he was coming to life, his finger was stuck in the trigger loop, and she couldn't pry it out, and she tried to point the gun at his head and pull the trigger but he opened his eyes blinking trying to wake up, and held his arm straight to the side, and he was getting stronger by the second.

"What the hell...?" he wondered and tried to get up, and tried to push Abby away while blinking his eyes.

Abby grabbed another rock and rushed to club him again but he blocked her arm and brought the gun up and fired and missed, shaking his head and trying to see straight while fending off the blows.

He fired again and the bullet whistled off a nearby tree.

Abby jumped up and ran, and when she looked back Philip was sitting upright and holding his jaw and yelling at her. "You can run, but you cannot hide! C'mon back and play some more love!"

She ran through the forest next to the steam. Nothing could help her now. She stumbled on a root and fell flat and twisted her knee, and she heard a cracking sound on the inside of it, and she cried out in pain and lay there for a moment out of breath with her face in the dirt. All was lost. Cree was dead, Jonah was most certainly dead, and she was not far behind them both. Pain throbbed in her knee but she didn't have time for it. She dragged herself back up and jumped into the stream, right into the center of the rapids that were heading down the valley. That's what Jonah had said they should do, ride the stream to the waterfall and take the cliff trail down and out of the valley. The water twisted at her and pulled her down and she struggled to stay afloat. Rocks crashed into her from all sides as she was swept down the rapids, and she swallowed some water and coughed it out while flailing her arms and then caught a branch hanging by the water's edge and held on for dear life.

'Dear life,' she thought, and nearly passed out from the pain and the cold water and despair. Dear sweet life.

All was lost. She gripped onto the slippery branch with both hands and put her cheek against the bark and green moss and closed her eyes. The river pulled at her and she felt her hands slipping and she tried to grasp harder but her strength was ebbing.

"Dear God," she whispered, "help me." It was the first time in her life that she had ever prayed, out loud that is, for she had secretly prayed in the past for small favors, getting a good grade, getting a good job, making it out of the submarine when it seemed they were going to die, prayed in silence so no one would hear her. And now hanging on, hanging on by a thread in a way, she whispered the prayer out loud again, the sound of it flowing over her lips like a melody.

"Dear God please help me."

She heard a cracking branch above and opened her eyes and looked up half expecting a miracle.

It was Philip looking down at her and grinning through blood stained teeth.

"Help me, help me," he mocked. "C'mon say it again, for me." And he laughed and it echoed throughout the valley. "Help me, help me!" He pointed the gun at her head and laughed. "Do you know what time it is?" He waited for the terror to spread across her face as he threatened her, but was disappointed.

Her life was over, it was finished, of that she was now sure, and that knowledge set her free. She was tired of running, tired of being afraid, and she smiled faintly. "You don't scare me anymore."

His left eye twitched, and he snarled and the spit and blood from his broken teeth and lips frothed from his mouth as he yelled, "It's time to die bitch!", and she gripped the branch even tighter, her expression calm even as she shivered with pain and cold.

The bear came silently behind Philip and stood on its hind legs towering over him. It had been feeding on salmon in the bushes nearby when it had been startled by all the yelling, and it had come to investigate, the pink flesh from the fish still dripping from its jaws. It was angry, and it roared, and it slapped Philip to the ground with a paw, and the hand gun clattered on the rocks. Philip looked up at the huge beast and tried to crawl backwards and away, and the bear jumped down on all fours again with his front feet crushing Philips chest and grabbed him by the head in his big slobbering jaws and half ripped it off crushing it like a melon while tearing at the body with its black claws.

It was a giant bear, huge and familiar, and she saw the white streak by its cheek and the softly furred ear with the perfect round notch from a recent bullet.

"Big Ben," she whispered as the bear mauled away.

Abby let go of the branch and drifted down the stream away from the carnage. The rapids eased and there was a calm part of the river and she swam to the shore and watched and listened.

A summer storm moved in and clouds filled the valley and a steady rain began to fall. After a while she climbed out of the water's edge and going far around in a big circle made her way back to where Jonah had fallen into the stream.

She searched for hours but couldn't find him, and slowly realized she never would. The river was now swollen from the rains and the water rushed angrily through the valley. It must have taken him away with it, she thought.

She stood there for a long time unable to move, numb, as though every bit of her being had been emptied out, all feelings hopes dreams and thoughts, everything including her will to live had been poured out of her, and she was alone, an empty shell.

"Jonah," she whispered, tears welling in her eyes and flowing down her cheeks. And then she made her way back to where Cree had fallen and covered his body in a mound of rocks and marked it with a cross made from pine branches.

34.

The blood red sun was setting low in the west as the two camels made their way across the desert, one following the other. The dry howling wind that had blown sand all day from the dunes into their eyes and ears was easing. The camels were struggling after the day long ride. White froth circled their mouths and noses and they snorted with exhaustion. The last time they drank water was from an oasis twenty miles back. The rider on the front camel sat upright, and looked back at the traveler on the rear horse and pointed in the direction they were headed.

"Hunaaka, hunaaka!" he yelled in Arabic over the wind. "There, there."

"Yes, yes I see it," whispered Abby beneath the veil. On the horizon loomed a row of oil derricks, their rigid sticks outlined in the orange sky like rocket ships poised for launch. She could see the pistons at the bases going up and down, up and down, pumping black crude from the depths. Off in the distance beyond the first line of rigs were many more, some with fire gushing from their tops as excess gas was burned off. They had made it, a five day trip across the most formidable desert in the world, the Rub' al Khali, the empty quarter, to the northern edge of the second largest known oil field in the world.

The Bedouins were rightly suspicious when she approached them last week in their village looking for a guide across the desert. No women in their part of the world were allowed to venture off on their own, and her story of being an archeologist raised eyebrows. There were no pharaoh's tombs or treasure in this desert, just hot sand. But she had cash money, and that was the deciding factor, ten thousand crisp American dollars sealed the deal.

Abby patted the bag at her side, and felt the stainless steel cylinder beneath the burlap. Filled with a quarter gallon of strain OE57, it was destined to be dropped into the first well she could find this very night. One hundred billion freeze dried spores would come to life in the rock and strata under the desert and spread throughout the depths and into every crack and crevice in the earth where oil existed in this part of the world, the colony of bacteria doubling every ten minutes until there was no more oil to eat. Within a year this entire oil field would be as dry as the desert that lay over it.

And before dawn she would head back on the route she came, like a wisp of wind in the night, and head to the next part of the globe, zigzagging across it. Europe, then Asia, South America, North America. Fifty cylinders like the one at her side had been shipped by mail throughout the world, and were waiting patiently at their destinations.

She would empty the reservoirs of oil all around the world; make them as empty as she was without Jonah. Humans would find something else to fight over, as they always did, but oil would be a thing of the past.

A bacterium was the first life on the planet, and would probably be the last. Mankind was the new kid on the block and what a strange misnomer that is, she thought, man and kind. How those two words ever got tangled up was a mystery.

And then she thought of Jonah, his funny face as she struggled to land the trout when they were hiding in Canada. The silly jokes, the way he talked about his family, the way he seemed so calm with the threat of the bear, repairing the plane with bark from a tree, the peace that seemed to envelope him as he sat in the shade of a pine tree and surveyed the nature that surrounded them when they had nowhere else to go, lost in the wilderness. Now that was a kind man.

High in the sky the sunlight reflected on the fuselage of a large airliner in the stratosphere as it flew on a steady course towards the West, and she watched as it faded out of sight. Then she brought her calm eyes down and focused her vision on the oil fields ahead, and listened to the harsh breathing of the camel, and the hooves hitting the sand.